"You don't have to clutch at me."

Amanda was playing it cool as she followed Piers into his hotel room. "If you want to talk, we'll talk."

"So tell me," he said, "why the sudden departure for home?"

"It isn't sudden," she lied. "I booked days ago."

"Liar!" he exclaimed. "The moment you told me you were going back to England and then said you knew my engagement was phony, I knew you were running away. I believe your engagement to Lucien was a phony as mine was to Helene and made for similar reasons."

"Don't play games with me anymore," he murmured softly. "Our marriage— and we are going to be married— must be a partnership, not a contest!"

ROBERTA LEIGH wrote her first book at the age of nineteen and since then has written more than seventy romance novels, as well as many books and film series for children. She has also been an editor of a women's magazine and produced a teen magazine, but writing romance fiction remains one of her greatest joys. She lives in Hampstead, London, and has one son.

Books by Roberta Leigh

LOVE WATCH

HARLEQUIN PRESENTS
169—CUPBOARD LOVE
175—MAN WITHOUT A HEART
182—UNWILLING BRIDEGROOM
193—TOO YOUNG TO LOVE
204—GIRL FOR A MILLIONAIRE
233—NOT A MARRYING MAN
461—CONFIRMED BACHELOR
819—NO TIME FOR MARRIAGE

HARLEQUIN ROMANCE
1696—MY HEART'S A DANCER
1715—IN NAME ONLY
1783—CINDERELLA IN MINK
1800—SHADE OF THE PALMS
1893—IF DREAMS CAME TRUE

These books may be available at your local bookseller.

Don't miss any of our special offers. Write to us at the following address for information on our newest releases.

Harlequin Reader Service
901 Fuhrmann Blvd., P.O. Box 1397, Buffalo, NY 14240
Canadian address: P.O. Box 603,
Fort Erie, Ont. L2A 5X3

ROBERTA LEIGH

maid to measure

Harlequin Books

TORONTO • NEW YORK • LONDON
AMSTERDAM • PARIS • SYDNEY • HAMBURG
STOCKHOLM • ATHENS • TOKYO • MILAN

Harlequin Presents first edition February 1987
ISBN 0-373-10954-7

Original hardcover edition published in 1986
by Mills & Boon Limited

CHAPTER ONE

THE tall, good-looking man leaned nonchalantly against the marble mantelpiece, one arm resting upon it, the other poised mid-air, a glass of whisky in hand. His dark, brooding presence dominated the elegant French boudoir, his six foot of highly tuned muscle and bone contrasting sharply with the gilded furniture and lacy fripperies.

'*You want me to marry Amanda Herbert?*' Piers Dubray's sapphire-blue eyes mirrored incredulity. 'Someone I haven't seen since she was thirteen?'

'It would be an ideal solution to an embarrassing situation,' his mother replied.

'It's not my fault I'll inherit Henry's title,' Piers said vehemently, 'so you can't talk me into inheriting his hideous daughter!'

'She might have improved by now. She was at the awkward age when you saw her.'

'It's no go, Maman. Anyway, I always regarded the idea of my marrying her as a joke.'

'Well, in a way it was, but with an underlying hope to it. Amanda's their only child and they're concerned for her future and her home.'

'I can't see why. She won't be short of money.' Piers raked a hand through his black curly hair, and his eyes—which earlier had been filled with amusement—sobered as he saw his mother's expression.

'It's more than a question of money,' she stated. 'Herbert House has been in their family for generations, and knowing it's entailed to you and that Amanda will have to move out when her father dies . . .'

'I still refuse to tie myself to a girl I barely know.'

'Then meet her again. It was such a pity you missed her twenty-first birthday party last year.'

'We were in California.'

'You could easily have flown back for it if you'd wanted to. So at least humour me by going to see her this weekend. You can't form an opinion until you have.'

'I formed my opinion eight years ago.' Piers' sensuous mouth, with its full lower lip, firmed into a straight line. 'She was an ugly little girl then, and I've no doubt she's an ugly big one now!'

'Margaret says she's lovely.'

'What else would you expect a mother to say?' Piers chuckled. 'You should have seen those eyes of hers, Maman. All set to follow me—one in each direction I went!'

His mother couldn't help smiling. 'They do wonders for squints these days.'

'And for figures? Hers would make a stick insect look shapely!'

'She was only thirteen, for goodness' sake—she's bound to have filled out! Anyway, Margaret assures me she's beautiful and intelligent. Has a degree in English, I believe, and works for a magazine.'

'A blue stocking. That's even worse!' Piers dug his hands into the pockets of his trousers, the stretched material hugging his well-muscled thighs. 'Look, Maman, I appreciate why you're keen on the idea, but, as I've said, I didn't ask to inherit Henry's title or that barn of a house. My home is here—this château.'

There was pride in his voice as he crossed to the window and stared out at the rolling green lawns which, fifty yards on, gave way to the deeper green of vineyards. In profile he appeared younger than his thirty-three years, his skin unlined, his chin—with its attractive cleft—firm as a rock. The sparkling glint in his eyes, the sensual curve of his mouth indicated a man who played, but was not to be played with.

'It's taken me twelve years to produce some of the best wine in the Loire,' he went on soberly, 'and it now looks as if our Napa Valley winery will soon be rivalling it. So what do I want with a house and land in England?'

'Give it to your children.'

'When and if I have any, they'll have their work cut out managing this little lot!' He turned back to the room. 'People aren't chess pieces to be pushed around, Maman, and I've no intention of tying myself to a girl I don't love.' The hectic flush on his mother's face—sure sign of her racing heart—made him soft-pedal a bit. 'Tell you what, though. I'll spend a weekend with Henry before the summer's over, and make it clear to him—as tactfully as possible, I promise—that I'm too much of a rake to be suitable for his darling daughter.'

'Amanda may not take to *you*,' his mother interposed, her doting expression clearly belying her comment.

'In which case honour will be satisfied and your conscience can rest easy!' her son declared. 'In fact, I'll ask Lucien to come with me. With a bit of luck they might fall for one another!'

Madame Dubray laughed. 'If they do, Amanda will get someone better natured than you. Your trouble is that you're wretchedly handsome and dreadfully spoiled because of it!'

'Then I'll behave true to form and not listen to you!' Piers bent to kiss his mother's brow, his dark curls a foil for her silver ones. 'Now no more talk of this ludicrous marriage, eh?'

'But you will go over for a weekend?'

'Yes. If only to stop Henry and Margaret counting chickens that have no chance of being hatched through me!'

His mother smiled, though it turned to a sigh as he sauntered out. Children! she thought with loving forbearance. What a trial they were!

CHAPTER TWO

'YOU can't be serious!' Amanda's auburn hair practically danced with astonishment. '*Me* marry Piers Dubray? Why, I haven't seen him since I was a kid!'

'You thought him very charming then,' her mother replied reasonably, 'and he can't have changed much. Anyway, he'll be here next weekend, so you can judge him for yourself.'

Amanda remembered the puppy love she had bestowed on her handsome third cousin when he had spent a summer holiday with them to inspect the stately home he would eventually inherit.

'I know you and Dad often talked about us marrying,' she went on, 'but I thought you were joking.'

'We were, but ...' Margaret Herbert looked frankly at her daughter. 'It would be so suitable, darling. You love this house, and if you and Piers made a match of it, it could still be your home.' She paused. 'But not if you don't love him, of course. Though he's so good-looking and intelligent, most women would give their eyeteeth for him.'

'Particularly the married ones,' Amanda said drily. 'I gather he's very partial to those.'

'You shouldn't believe everything you read. You know how scandalous French magazines can be. Anyway, Eliana wrote saying how fondly he remembers you.'

Not to mention how fondly he remembers my money, Amanda thought, but, not wishing to upset her mother, she said instead, 'You don't fall for someone simply because they're good-looking and intelligent. Not even scientists know what attracts one

8

person to another. They think it has something to do with pheromones and——'

'Spare me all that jargon,' her mother interrupted. 'You're not writing one of your articles now!'

'Which reminds me, I've a deadline to meet. I was late last week, and Liz got quite stroppy.'

'I haven't finished talking to you,' Margaret Herbert insisted.

But Amanda's long, shapely legs were already taking her to the door. Marry Piers Dubray? She'd rather stay single the rest of her life! If there was one type of man she couldn't abide, it was a philanderer—and Piers took first prize!

She half-smiled as she remembered how she'd drooled over him during his two weeks' stay; trailing after him like a lovesick puppy and getting ecstatic whenever he flashed his dimpled smile at her. At least she was well over *that*. Which brought her back to this stupid marriage arrangement.

Her mother had told her several years ago that Piers had retrieved the family fortune which his father's bungling had depleted, but she was still convinced that her attraction for him lay with her own considerable inheritance rather than her charms. He was a Latin, after all, and weren't they notorious for marrying for money and having a mistress on the side?

Still, it would be fun seeing him again. And even funnier when he saw how she'd changed. Her soft mouth curved in a smile as she remembered how plain and gawky she had been. But beanpole skinny had transformed itself to tall and willowy, carroty frizz had softened to auburn waves, and crooked teeth and squint had happily been corrected, so that instead of being a head-turner for all the wrong reasons she was now a head-turner for all the right ones!

'So when's pretty boy arriving?' she asked, her hand on the door-knob.

'Friday. And *do* be nice to him, dear. Eliana's one of my dearest friends.'

'You haven't seen her in years.'

'Only because she spends so much time in California with Piers—Amanda, will you listen to me?'

'Later, Ma. I've work to do.'

Friday came, the article was duly sent off, and Amanda—though reluctant to admit it even to herself—was quite excited at the prospect of meeting the man she had once had an adolescent crush on. She had been somewhat surprised to learn he was bringing a friend and, for the first time, wondered if Piers was as wary of meeting her as she of meeting him.

She was still mulling this over when Mandy, who came in to help when they had visitors, burst into her sitting-room to say the two Frenchmen had arrived.

'Did you manage to see them?' Amanda asked.

'I'll say! And they're both eye-catching—especially your cousin. At least, I'm pretty sure it was him from the way the Earl thumped his back.' Mandy rolled her eyes heavenwards. 'I'd work here full time if I knew *he* was going to be around.' She clapped a hand to her mouth. 'Sorry. I didn't mean——'

'Forget it,' Amanda said. 'Though I must say it gives me the creeps to think of *that* creep waiting on the sidelines to step into my father's shoes . . .' Pushing the thought away, she switched off her hair drier. 'I wouldn't mind having a peep at our visitors before I actually meet them. If you could find out where they go after they've unpacked, I might be able to manage it.'

'Will do!' Mandy said cheerily, and bounced out, returning some quarter of an hour later to say they were having a drink on the terrace.

Slipping into a dark green dress with a matching scarf to hide her hair—it would make her less visible in the bushes that were to be her cover—Amanda crept down the back stairs and out of the side of the house.

Stealthily crouching low, she inched forward and saw the two men sitting at the table. They were deep in conversation, and, moving closer, she settled in the middle of a huge clump of rhododendrons, so thick and dense that even at a few paces she wasn't visible.

Anxious to get a better look at them, she carefully tilted a branch aside.

Her breath caught in her throat! She was confronted by the most devastatingly handsome man she had ever seen. That it was Piers, she knew instantly, and the teenage crush she had thought lost in the mists of memory was stirred to life by the powerful sensuousness of a tall, lean body and aggressively masculine features. Slowly her eyes took in the long, aristocratic nose above a wide, well-cut mouth, the high cheekbones lending hauteur to a sun-bronzed face, and beautifully arched black eyebrows over astonishingly deep blue eyes.

For a moment longer she feasted her eyes on him, aware of a vulnerability in her that she had never experienced before, then reluctantly turned her attention to his friend.

Talk about a contrast! Apart from the fact that they were similar in build, the other man was as blond as Piers was dark, his hair the gold of a newly minted penny, with eyes almost to match. His features were softer, too, and she judged him to be far less complex a character.

All in all, they were two handsome specimens of manhood, guaranteed to stir every female pulse, Piers in shades of blue that indicated an awareness of what it did for his eyes, his friend in impeccably cut brown slacks and matching silk sweater.

'I still don't know why you brought me here!' Piers' friend was saying in swift, Parisian French, which Amanda could follow perfectly.

'To watch me act the dutiful son, and plight my troth to the lovely Amanda.'

A shout of laughter greeted this. 'Plight your troth be darned! I can't see you giving up your bachelor status for *any* woman!'

'That's what I told Maman, but she wouldn't listen. So to appease her I consented to come over and meet the girl, as well as to introduce you, my friend, to one of the prettiest young ladies in England.'

Amanda smiled happily. Who said eavesdroppers never heard good of themselves? But her elation was short lived, as Piers spoke again.

'Don't look so pleased, old friend. If Amanda's as hideous today as she was at thirteen ...' He sighed heavily and crossed one long leg over the other. 'Mothers can be the devil!'

'Maybe the girl's improved.'

'How do you improve buck teeth and a squint?'

'Difficult,' Lucien agreed. 'So how are you going to handle the situation?'

'With my usual charm and tact. I'll make it perfectly clear to her parents that, though I find their daughter delightful, I have no intention of marrying *anyone* in the foreseeable future.'

'It's fatal to tell a female you aren't the marrying kind,' Lucien said instantly. 'It's like waving a red flag to a bull! The harder-to-get you play, the harder she'll come after you.'

'Then what about——?' Piers cogitated. 'What about my saying I'm entering a monastery?'

His companion gave a roar of laughter. 'A convent, more like it!'

Piers chuckled, and Amanda, fuming in her leafy hideout, contemplated every exquisite way of torturing this arrogant swine. Buck teeth and squint, eh! Wait till she laid her hands on him. She'd tear him limb from handsome limb!

'Seriously, Piers,' Lucien was speaking again. 'If

this unfortunate girl's as plain as you say, maybe it would have been kinder if you'd stayed away.'

'I tell you I couldn't get out of it! But one thing for sure, the quicker this weekend's over the better!'

A chair scraped on the flagstones, and through the leaves Amanda saw Piers get to his feet. He was, if anything, even more impressive, with a wide-shouldered ranginess that indicated prime physical condition. I'm surveying him as if he's meat on a butcher's slab, she thought, and barely restrained a chuckle. After all, that was how he regarded *her*. Except that he'd made it clear he wasn't buying in any circumstances! Which of course was precisely what she herself had said to her mother!

Lucien rose too, and the two men strolled along the terrace and into the drawing-room, leaving Amanda cogitating among the rhododendrons.

Honesty made her admit that at thirteen she'd been no Raquel Welch, but she hadn't been Miss Dracula either! Unexpectedly she giggled at the thought of making this gorgeous hunk eat his words. Oh yes. She'd teach Piers Dubray a lesson he'd never forget!

Making certain the coast was clear, she crept from the bushes and rushed up to her mother's bedroom, where she found her sitting at her dressing-table, twisting her long blonde hair into a chignon. Seeing her daughter's face in the mirror, pink-cheeked with excitement, Margaret Herbert swivelled round.

'What is it, dear?'

'I've just been listening to Piers.' Without pause for breath, Amanda recounted all she had overheard, and was somewhat put out when her mother's initial indignation gave way to bubbling laughter.

'Serves you right for eavesdropping! Anyway, he was right. You were a most unprepossessing teenager.'

'But not the Medusa he described,' Amanda said crossly.

'One can't expect a man of—what was he then—

twenty-four, twenty-five?—to see the swan in the ugly
duckling.' Her mother's wide-set grey eyes—so like
her daughter's—moved from the wavy, dark auburn
hair and heart-shaped face to the tall, slender body.
'And you are definitely a swan, my darling, as Piers
will soon see for himself. It's my bet he'll sink at your
feet!'

'And lick them probably! But it won't do him any
good. I've no intention of being nice to that
supercilious, conceited——'

'Devastating and sexy——'

'Mother!'

'Well, he is! I may be fifty, but I'm not blind! I
know you're upset, darling, but you can't exactly
blame him. Anyway, once you meet, It won't mean a
thing.'

'You didn't *hear* him,' Amanda said mutinously.

'I know, but treat it as a joke. Just think how
startled he'll be when he actually sees you again. I
mean, the whole purpose of this visit is for you two to
meet each other.' Her mother broke off, aware of her
daughter's eyes sparkling so brilliantly that they
appeared silver. 'Amanda—you're plotting something!
I don't like the look on your face.'

'Piers will like it even less,' said her daughter,
walking excitedly around the room. 'I've just dreamed
up the perfect way of paying him back.'

'I don't think I want to hear,' the Countess said
standing up and reaching for her dress. 'In fact, I
definitely don't.'

'You'll have to, Ma. I need your help.'

'No, Amanda.'

Amanda's look was so pleading that her mother's
resolve wavered and she sat down again. 'Well, what is it?'

Quickly Amanda explained, and though to begin
with Margaret Herbert looked askance, her sense of
humour soon got the better of her discretion, which
was exactly what Amanda had hoped.

'It would be hilarious if it worked,' her mother agreed reluctantly, 'but I can't see your getting away with it.'

'Why not? Didn't I always play the lead in the school plays?'

'That was different. This isn't an act on a stage.'

'All the world's a stage,' Amanda put in. 'Look, Ma, all I want is to give him a fright. First I'll let him see me looking hideous, then after he's stewed a bit I'll come down to dinner in all my stunning glory.'

'I must say it's an amusing idea,' her mother agreed, stepping into her dress.

'Then call Dad and tell him I have the measles.'

'The measles? Is that really necessary?' Seeing her daughter's face, Margaret Herbert resignedly lifted the intercom beside her bed.

'Henry? Something dreadful's happened. Amanda's got measles.'

'I knew it,' the Earl's voice boomed down the receiver. 'The new stable lad's gone down with it, and she was riding with him a few days ago. But hang on. Didn't she have measles the winter we went to St Moritz?'

With her ear pressed to the phone, Amanda mouthed at her mother.

'That was *German* measles, Henry,' his wife lied.

'Hmph!' the Earl grunted. 'Well, that puts paid to her meeting Piers—unless he's already had it!'

'Had it or not, she won't see him while she looks such a fright.'

'Twaddle! A couple of spots won't scare him off.'

Amanda shook her head vehemently and her mother spoke again.

'No, Henry. She absolutely *won't* see him until she's better.'

'Obstinate girl,' the Earl said despondently. 'Can't think where she gets it from.'

'Your mother, I should think,' his wife replied.

'You'd best have a word with Piers, then,' her husband went on, ignoring her comment. 'Tell him he can leave after dinner if he likes.'

'I don't think that's very polite, dear. We'll let him decide for himself.'

Replacing the receiver, Margaret gave her daughter a conspiratorial smile. 'You know, I'm beginning to enjoy this little game.'

'I knew you would. Now all you've got to do is call Piers.'

With far more confidence, her mother did, and Amanda listened on tenterhooks as his voice, deep and sexy, echoed through the room.

'How disappointing,' he said, his English only faintly accented. 'And I was so looking forward to meeting your lovely daughter.'

'Amanda's devastated too,' his hostess replied, then after a suitable pause, 'but there's no reason why you can't get a glimpse of each other.'

'A glimpse?'

'Yes, dear boy.' The Countess—like her daughter— was hard put to stifle her laughter. 'If you go into the rose garden in about half an hour and look up at the first floor window, Amanda will wave down to you.'

'What a charming idea. Then afterwards, if you will excuse us, Lucien and I will return to London. With Amanda indisposed, you won't want to be bothered with guests.'

'Not at all. It's delightful having you. Do stay overnight, Piers, and leave in the morning. I'm only upset you've had a wasted journey.'

'A glimpse of Amanda through the window won't make it wasted,' Piers said in a tone of such deep insincerity that Amanda backed away from the telephone in case he heard her laughter.

'Me at thirteen will have been a raving beauty compared with what he's going to see in half an hour!' she said as the call ended.

'What are you going to do to yourself?'

'I'm not sure. But it won't be a pretty sight!'

'You must look your best at dinner,' her mother insisted.

'I promised I would, so quit worrying.'

Some twenty minutes later, peeping from behind her bedroom drapes, Amanda saw Piers stroll into the rose garden. He seemed oblivious of the colourful blooms with their heady scent, his attention riveted on the first floor window, and she moved closer to the glass and pulled the drapes apart.

His instant, horrified recoil was exactly what she had hoped for, and she dug her nails into her palms to keep herself from having hysterics. She'd got Medusa to a 'T'!

An orange frizz of hair stuck out from the mauve scarf she had tied tightly around her pallid, spotty face—courtesy of talcum powder and Max Factor lipstick. Large, crooked teeth loomed out of a mouth that made the Grand Canyon seem small, while black-rimmed pebble lenses caught the rays of the setting sun.

'Too bad about the measles!' she trilled in an accent as polished as cut glass. 'But I hope we can meet in France when I'm better.'

'I'm off to California any day now,' he said in a choked voice.

'When you get back, then.'

'It may be months.'

'Never mind. I might fly out there and surprise you!' Amanda gave a horsey whinny of excitement and leaned further out to show him her ample bosom—a stick insect, he'd called her, and to confound him she had padded herself fat as a pregnant cow!

'Have you had the measles, Piers?' she screeched.

'I—er—why?'

'Because if you have, you can come up and see me. You can't get it twice.'

'I've never had it once,' he called hastily. 'And please don't stand at the window too long or you'll catch cold.'

'How darling of you to be so concerned,' she neighed. 'I do wish I could be with you.'

'Me too,' he lied, backing away.

'What are you going to do now?' she demanded, resting her 'pillow breasts' on the sill for him to see.

'Take a walk in the woods until dinner,' he replied in strangled tones. 'Adieu, Amanda. I wish you better.'

Quickly turning on his heel, he strode off as though the devil were after him, leaving Amanda to collapse on a chair and laugh until she cried.

CHAPTER THREE

ONCE she had caught her breath, Amanda spat out the orange peel 'teeth' she had tucked carefully behind her lips, and plucked the orange feathers from her hair, while Mandy—still doubled up with laughter— attempted to stick them back in the now sadly depleted feather duster.

'Did you see his *face*?' Amanda choked. 'His horrified expression?'

'I think the sight of you will haunt him for the rest of his life,' Mandy giggled. 'Pity the lesson can't go on.'

A speculative gleam came into Amanda's grey eyes. 'Maybe it can. As you say, it's a shame to let him off the hook so easily.' Quickly she dipped her fingers into a jar of cleansing cream and plastered it over her lipstick-daubed face.

'What do you have in mind?' Mandy asked.

'Nothing yet. I'm still thinking.'

Tissue poised, Amanda sauntered back to the window, as if the answer lay below her in the rose garden. But all she saw was a blaze of colour, and Piers walking towards the dark green stretch of the woods beyond.

'I've got it!' she cried, swivelling round. 'Now listen carefully.'

Mandy's startled 'Ohs' and 'Ahs' turned to excited anticipation as Amanda's scheme unfolded. 'It's a smashing idea, but do you think you can carry it off?'

'Sure I can. But we must hurry or I'll miss him.'

Two minutes later a giggling Mandy, wrapped in Amanda's housecoat, scurried from the room, while Amanda quickly donned the girl's navy dress and white apron. This time she made herself up differently—not the clown she had been at the window, but still fairly heavy with the lipstick and blusher, and lavish with the eye make-up. Only with her hair did she really go to town, teasing the soft waves into a bouffant frizz that made it stand out as if electrified, then carefully spraying on gold glitter that turned the auburn to carrot.

Surveying herself in the mirror, she was highly delighted. Five feet eight without shoes, and slenderly formed, with full breasts, she was the direct opposite of Mandy, who was five feet three and flat-chested, so that the cotton uniform fitted only where it touched, which wasn't in all that many places! Still, it was exactly right for what she was planning, and filled with pleasurable anticipation she sprinted down the back stairs and out to the woods.

It was cool and pleasant there after the heat of the day, and stealthily—like a tigress stalking its victim— she crept towards the clearing where she had seen Piers heading.

She found him perched on a fallen log, his back to her, idly flipping pebbles at a beech tree a few yards away.

Amanda's heart did such silly flip flops at the sight of him that she almost gave up her plan. But remembering the needlessly cruel things he had said about her, she mustered the courage to smooth down her clinging dress and wiggle provocatively towards him.

He turned sharply as a twig snapped at her approach, his eyes running over her assessingly, making her embarrassingly aware of her skimpy garment. Blow Mandy! Why couldn't she have been six inches taller!

Aloud, she feigned a higher tone than normal and a slight cockney accent. 'Afternoon, sir.'

'Good afternoon.' Staying where he was, his eyes

continued to range over her body with frank and insolent admiration.

Some manners he's got! Amanda thought, giving his slouching form a withering look. As though sensing her derision, he rose slowly, and as she watched the rugged frame unfurl, an unaccustomed sense of fragility swamped her. Even in her bare feet she wasn't used to looking up to any man; yet despite the flat shoes she had donned—as befitted her status of parlour-maid—she found herself doing exactly that!

'Mind if I rest me pins?' she asked, and, not waiting for an answer, dropped to the grass.

'Be my guest,' he said, flashing her a devastating smile as he resumed his place on the log, legs outstretched.

'I suppose you work at Herbert House,' he stated, nodding towards her uniform.

'Yes. I just sneaked away from that bad-tempered little bitch!'

He looked startled. 'What bitch?'

'Lady A., who else? She's in one of her foul moods again, what with getting the measles and not being able to meet that gigolo who's come specially to see her . . .'

'Gigolo?' Piers' eyes narrowed.

'Yes. Some Frenchman who's after her money. Not that he stands much chance of getting it. She had a good look at him from the window and didn't fancy what she saw. Said all he needed was longer hair and he could've passed for a girl!'

'Indeed.' A flush darkened Pier's tan, and Amanda was hard put to keep a straight face.

'And the *clothes* he wore!' she giggled, warming to her role. 'Lady A. said he was togged out as if he was going to a party, instead of spending a weekend in a country house.'

'I see.' Piers' mouth thinned with anger and he flung a stone violently at the beech tree.

'So all in all,' Amanda went on relentlessly, 'it don't look as if he'll get to first base with her. Pretty boy blue she called him!'

This was too much for Piers, and he jumped up.

'I'd best be going too,' she said casually, but as she rose his hands shot out to grip her shoulders. A delicious warmth spread through her at his touch and she tried to pull free, irritated with herself for her reaction.

'Don't be scared,' he said gently. 'I won't hurt you. All I want is your honest opinion.'

'About what?'

'Whether *you* think I'm effeminate.'

'You, sir?' Her eyes widened in mock astonishment. 'You mean—oh, you *can't* be Lady Amanda's Frenchman!'

'I am, and I'm still waiting for your answer.'

Tilting her head, she took her time studying him, an expression of intense concentration on her face.

'Well?' he repeated edgily. 'What's your verdict?'

'I think you're smashing,' Amanda said bluntly. 'Quite fanciable, in fact. Oh, Lord!' She clapped her hand to her mouth. 'Don't let on I've been talking to you like this or I'll lose me job.'

'I won't breathe a word.' He dropped his hands. 'I don't give a damn what Amanda thinks of me. In fact, she's probably too blind to see much anyway!'

Well, *I'm* not blind, Amanda thought mutinously, and I can see very well what a swine you are! How quickly he had recovered from her insulting description of him! Yet with so many women swooning at his feet, who could blame him?

'How long have you been working here?' he asked unexpectedly. 'A pretty girl like you shouldn't be stuck out in the country.'

'I know.' She gave another high-pitched giggle. 'But jobs are hard to find these days.'

He gave a devilish grin. 'I might be able to help you.'

'Doing what?'

'That's something we'd have to talk over.'

Amanda seethed. 'If you're implying what I think you are, sir, you can go jump in the lake!'

'Hey, I was paying you a compliment!'

'A back-handed one, which I can do without. I ain't easy game, you know!'

He had the grace to look apologetic. 'Sorry. All I meant was that you're a very pretty young lady. I'd no ulterior motive, I assure you. I prefer my women sophisticated.'

'Then how come you were considering marrying Lady A.?'

'I wasn't. I'd rather be a monk than tied to that gargoyle!' He moving restlessly around the clearing. 'Trouble is, as long as I'm unattached, my mother won't give up on the idea.'

'She might even wear you down in the end,' Amanda said solemnly.

'Not a chance.' Abruptly he stopped walking and gave her a penetrating stare.

'Why are you looking at me like that?' she asked.

'Because you've just given me an idea.'

'I ain't said nothing!'

He went on staring at her. 'If I could find myself a temporary fiancée, it would put paid to my mother's plans.'

'It sure would. Except that once you were free again, she'd start nagging.'

'It would at least give me a respite. I'd remain engaged until I went to California—I usually spend several months at a time there—and when I return I'll make out I'm still nursing a broken heart.' He chuckled. 'It's the best solution I've come up with so far. All I have to do is find a suitable girl.'

'You're so handsome,' Amanda said sarcastically, 'that shouldn't be any problem.'

'You're right. I've already found her.'

'Who?'

'*You.*'

'You're crazy!' Amanda thought his idea of a phoney engagement a clever suberfuge, but couldn't see why he needed the help of an unknown girl he had just met.

'You must know loads of French girls who'd jump at the chance,' she insisted.

'Dozens,' he agreed. 'But I'd have a hell of a problem getting rid of them at the end! Women tend to be possessive over me,' he added so nonchalantly that if Amanda had had a pin she would have stuck it in him!

'What makes you think I'll be different?' she demanded.

'Even if you weren't, I'd know how to deal with you.' Playfully he cuffed her cheek. 'Come now, what have you got to lose?'

'My job for a start. I won't get it back if I walk out.'

'You won't need it any more. I'll make this one worth your while. Say a thousand pounds—and a few pleasant weeks passing as the light of my life.'

'Think a lot of yourself, don't you?' Amanda mocked, looking him up and down the way he had done her. 'I agree you're quite a looker, but you ain't my type.'

'That makes us both safe, then,' he said cheerfully.

'Oh? A minute ago you said I was pretty.'

'So you are.' He gave her his most persuasive smile. 'But, as I said, I prefer my women sophisticated. Look, you'll be perfectly safe with me—and a deal of money richer—so why not help me out?'

It was a great temptation to accept, for she could see all sorts of possibilities in the situation, not least the marvellous one of making him look an absolute fool when she fianlly revealed her identity.

'Okay,' she said slowly. 'But I want two thousand quid.'

'That's pretty steep for a few months' work.'

'A few *months*?' Amanda was dismayed. She could play-act for a few days, a week even, but never for the length of time he was asking. 'I wouldn't stay for months,' she stated. 'That's out of the question.'

'Let's say one month, then,' came the hasty reply. 'All I'm asking for is time to convince my mother I'm in love with you . . . And for that, you'll have to stay with me at the château.'

'You'd better make it three thousand.'

'Hey! Every time you open your mouth, the price goes up.'

'Because every time you open yours, the job lengthens. And staying in your home with your mother won't be a picnic, you know. I'll have to be on guard the whole time.'

'You'll soon get used to it. And you'll enjoy yourself there.'

'I'll enjoy the money I get at the end of it.' She eyed him. 'Why do we have to stay at the château so long?'

'I've some work to catch up on there.'

'You mean you ain't a gentleman farmer?' Amanda asked guilelessly, and saw him hide a smile.

'I'm a viticulturist—a winegrower,' he explained. 'And this is an anxious time of year on the estate, watching the weather, the growth of the grapes . . . I may even need to be there with you for five weeks. And not a penny more,' he asserted as he saw her lips part. 'Take it or leave it.'

'I'll take it,' she said sullenly. 'But I want half now, and the rest when the job's done.'

'You're a tough taskmaster.'

'You're the master,' she retorted, 'but don't get any ideas about me ending up your mistress!'

'No fear of that,' he grunted. 'Let's shake on it.'

Slowly she gave him her hand, and with his spare one hand he tilted her face and stared into her deep grey eyes, his own sparkling like sapphires.

'I think a bit less muck on your face would be fine for a start,' he murmured.

A retort was ready on her lips, but she bit it back, knowing that if she wished to continue this charade that had fallen so unexpectedly into her lap, she had best play it carefully. What a story it would make for a woman's magazine!

'We leave for France first thing tomorrow morning,' he said, dropping her hand.

'So soon?' Amanda began to have cold feet again.

'With Lady Amanda ill, the Herberts won't want me hanging around.' His tone grew softer. 'Don't be afraid. You'll manage fine.'

Mulling over his words, she decided that even if her act was the flop of all time, it wouldn't be the end of the world. She'd just have to tell him the truth sooner rather than later.

And after that what? Would they part friends or enemies? But she refused to think beyond the next few weeks.

'So it's settled, then,' he said into the silence.

'I'm not sure, sir.' She gave a nervous giggle. 'I— er—I find you frightening.'

'Why?'

'Well, I've heard you're a playboy and——'

'Playboy?' he said in a tone of affront. 'I'll have you know I work damned hard, and—but why am I explaining myself to you? I'm paying you to play a part—not be my inquisitor!'

'I still have to know something about you—else why would I love you?'

'For my charm.'

'What charm?'

He laughed. 'Sharp, aren't you? What's your name?'

'Amanda,' she said without thinking, then, seeing his surprise, added quickly, 'A coincidence, ain't it? But everyone calls me Mandy.'

'Very well then, Mandy, I promise as soon as we

leave here, I'll fill you in on my lurid background!' He thought for a moment. 'I'll pick you up at the crossroads at nine-thirty tomorrow morning.'

'It's too far for me to walk with me cases,' Amanda said in a complaining voice. 'You'll have to come to the back door later tonight and collect them.'

'Very well. But don't let anyone see us.'

'Yes, sir,' she said meekly. 'Is there anything else?'

'No,' he said authoritatively. 'Damn it, yes, there is! Stop calling me "sir"—my name's Piers—and get rid of that hideous dark lipstick and try not to giggle so much.'

'I can't help it if I find you funny,' she sniffed. 'S'pose it's because you're a foreigner!'

'I won't be a foreigner when we get to France!' he said acidly, and before she could reply strode away without a backward glance.

Watching him, Amanda was uncertain where this jape of hers would lead, or precisely how it would end. She was deceiving not only Piers, but his mother too. And thinking of mothers, how would her own react to this latest turn of events?

'It's simply out of the question, Amanda,' came the positive assertion, some minutes later. 'Playing a trick on Piers was fine—he needed bringing down a peg—but I'm not happy about your misleading Eliana.'

'It won't be for long. And think of the fun it'll be!'

'Piers might be looking for fun too,' came the reply. 'He's the *last* man to turn my head!'

'It won't stop him trying. Anyway, I don't see the point of the exercise. You had your fun with him in the woods, and I think you should forget about doing anything more. Now get changed and come down to dinner as your real self.'

'Oh, Ma,' Amanda protested, 'it's time someone cut him down to size, and I've the perfect opportunity.'

'I can't stop you, my dear. You're over twenty-one.'

'But I won't do it if you disapprove. I just wish you

could have heard him this afternoon. He thinks he's God's gift to women.'

'Even so . . .' The Countess looked lovingly at her daughter's flashing eyes and dimpled, determined chin. 'Did you say it would only be for a few weeks?'

'Yes.' Amanda crossed her fingers.

'You won't do anything silly, will you?'

'You know me better than that.'

'All I know is that you always get round me,' Margaret Herbert sighed. 'What shall I tell your father this time?'

'That I've gone to Scandinavia to research a book.'

'Ever thought of taking up politics? You tell such beautiful lies!'

'Only white ones!'

'One thing, though,' her mother called after her as Amanda hurried from the room, 'if you let this charade go on too long, I'll put a stop to it.'

'Give me a month,' Amanda pleaded, 'and I promise I'll return, victorious.'

'And Piers?'

'He'll be nursing a broken ego and definitely contemplating the monastic life!'

CHAPTER FOUR

POWDER and paint, normally a girl's best friend, was hardly Amanda's next morning.

Thick black mascara spiked her long lashes, iridescent pink shadow glittered her lids, and scarlet blobs of colour marred each cheek. Envisaging Pier's horror at her interpretation of 'go easy on the make-up,' she grinned broadly as she drew a thick line of kohl round the rims of her grey eyes, and gave the delicate curves of her soft mouth a ferocious pout with a splosh of mauve lipstick, the bow at the centre of her upper lip extending well outside its normal, delicious outline.

'Think I'm overdoing it?' she asked her mother.

'That's the understatement of the year!'

'Good!' With a final tease of her carrot hair—its shining auburn now rinsed bright orange—Amanda stepped into three-inch, high-heeled gold sandals.

Her clothes for her newly acquired role had presented her with a problem, and only last-minute rummaging by Mandy in a trunkful of old dresses—kept for playing charades at Christmas—had solved her dilemma, for she had discovered a bright green satin jacket which she had cleverly converted into a tarty blouse, and a gaudy red skirt to wear with it.

'You look like a cockatoo!' Margaret Herbert chortled. 'I'd give anything to see Piers' face!'

'Or read his thoughts!' her daughter chuckled and, giving her mother a hug, she set off for the crossroads where she had arranged to meet Piers.

She found him tapping his fingers impatiently on the bonnet of his hired Ford, his tall frame elegant in navy slacks and navy and white silk shirt.

'You're late,' he grunted. 'Had trouble leaving?'

'Not really. I told the Countess my grandfather had been run over by a bus.'

'How original! You'll have to do better than that if you lie to *me*.'

'I'd never lie to *you*,' Amanda assured him.

'Damn right you wouldn't!' Piers swung round to his side of the car and slid behind the wheel, leaving her standing.

'If I'm supposed to be your fiancée,' she called, hands on hips, 'you should at least have the manners to open the door for me.'

'I'll start acting the part when you start looking it. I've never seen such a get-up!'

'I can't help the way I dress,' she whined. 'I ain't got much money and——'

'Half the girls I know don't have much money,' he cut in, 'but they don't look like Christmas crackers! And didn't I tell you to go easy on the make-up?'

'I'd feel funny without it.'

'You look even funnier with it! Oh, get in the car and I'll sort you out later.'

Catching a glimpse of herself in the side mirror as she climbed in, she bit back a smile. Her little game had got off to a flying start!

'Where's your friend?' she asked as they set off down the narrow country lane.

'He left last night.'

'Why?'

'Because he doesn't approve of what I intend doing with you.'

His friend soared sharply in Amanda's estimation, but she was careful not to show it. 'What do you mean by "intend doing with me"?' she asked in a high-pitched voice. 'If you've any funny ideas——'

'Be quiet!' he roared. 'This is a business transaction, pure and simple. A bit too simple, if you ask me,' he added, giving her a sour glance. 'The original idea was to take you straight to the château, but if my mother sees the way you look she'll think I've gone out of my head. We'll have to stop in Paris and get you something decent to wear.'

'Watch your tongue,' Amanda said heatedly. 'I won't be spoken to like what I was dirt.'

'As *if* I was dirt,' he corrected. 'Didn't they teach you grammar at school?'

'It was me worst subject. But I'm bloody marvellous at carpentry.'

'How useful,' he said smoothly. 'Though I'd be obliged if you'd cut out the "bloodies". Ladies don't swear.'

'You ain't heard Lady Amanda. The other day she called me a——'

'I don't wish to hear,' he cut in. 'You're working for me now, so forget about her.'

Amanda nodded and peered at herself in the mirror, taking a large comb from her purse to tease the front of her hair.

'Don't do that,' Piers ordered. 'It's back-combed to hell as it is.'

'Gentlemen don't swear,' she said so pertly that he laughed.

'Sorry, Mandy. I'd forgotten how sharp you were.'

'Sharp enough to want half me money on account.'

'Don't you trust me?'

'I don't trust anyone.'

'Been hurt, have you?'

She nodded, then proceeded to invent a sob story. 'Me father left home when I was three, and me stepfather was a drunk.'

'*My* stepfather.'

'You got one also?' she asked guilelessly.

'What? No, of course not! All I meant was—hell! I——'

'Gentlemen don't——'

'Swear,' he finished for her. 'Okay. I won't swear if you'll stop saying "me" instead of "my".'

'I can't say what I ain't used to.'

'Aren't,' he said heavily.

'And uncle to you!' she flared. 'If you can't take me like I am, let's call it a day. Anyway, posh accents don't matter these days. It's what you have up here that counts.' She tapped her forehead. 'And I got plenty.'

'I'm sure you have,' Piers reassured her, 'and I stand duly corrected. Your accent's a delight, and if my mother remarks on it I'll tell her they speak that way in Gloucestershire!'

'So you'll take me as I am?' Amanda demanded.

'Yes. Except for the small matter of a new wardrobe and hairstyle.'

'Like Eliza in *My Fair Lady*?' she giggled. 'I saw it on telly the other night and it was smashing!'

Piers muttered beneath his breath, and Amanda lapsed into silence, deciding she had teased him enough for the moment. Besides, if she overdid it, he might get cold feet and pay her off, and she wasn't ready to say goodbye to him yet.

'I assume you don't speak French?' he asked abruptly.

''Fraid not.' She gave him a winsome smile and, batting her lashes at him, saw him swallow.

'Would you please remove those long black spider legs you've stuck around your eyes?' he asked in a thin voice.

'I can't. They're me own!'

'You mean they're real?'

'Right. Long, ain't they?'

He looked flummoxed. 'Look, I don't mean to upset you, but your eyes are lovely enough without all that goo on them.'

'I'm ever so pleased you think so,' she giggled raucously, hiding her mirth as he swore quietly but forcibly in French. What she would have given to see his face if she replied to him in his own language!

'How long will we be in Paris?' she asked after they reached Heathrow and he checked in the car.

'As long as it takes to make you look less—er—colourful.'

'You ain't half a nag,' she said with feigned petulance as they entered the terminal.

'I have to be. It's imperative you at least *look* as if I could be in love with you.'

She ignored this. 'What hotel are we staying in?'

'I have an apartment in Paris.' He held out his hand as they moved to the check-in counter. 'Your passport, please.'

Realising the game would be up if he saw it, she shook her head. 'I'll book myself in, thanks. I'm not a dummy. Just give me my ticket.'

Irritably he complied, and after checking in she darted ahead of him through passport control, breathing a sigh of relief as she slipped her passport back into her purse. She only hoped she wouldn't have the same trouble at the other end!

Unfortunately she did, but pretending she was examining a run in her tights, she managed to lag sufficiently behind Piers for him not to see her passport when she presented it.

His car—a champagne-coloured Maserati—was parked at the airport, and in no time they were in Paris and cruising along the Champs Elysées.

Amanda had no need to feign delight at the sight of this famous avenue, or surprise when they reached a smart apartment block off the Place de la Concorde. Not bad for a hard-up playboy, she mused as the elevator took them up to the second floor and they walked into his surprisingly opulent home.

Georgian-green silk lined the walls of the hall and living-room, where matching drapes fell in folds to a parquet floor scattered with washed Chinese rugs. The antique furniture was culled from various periods: Napoleonic desk, Directoire chairs and tables, gilt-framed Louis Seize settees, their taut springs replaced by down-filled cushions of lemon velvet.

Her bedroom—to which an elderly, poker-faced housekeeper escorted her—was eclectic too, with a marquetry dressing-table and chairs and a mahogany French Empire bed, the pink and gold damask coverlet echoing the fabric lining the walls. Thick carpeting underfoot—in pink and gold again—swept through to a circular bathroom, where a pink marble tub with gold dolphin faucets proclaimed the newest decorator fashion.

Piers certainly catered to the women in his life, Amanda mused, and tried picturing his tall, lean frame in this nest of pleasure. Returning to the bedroom, she cautiously peered into the corridor. It was empty, and curiosity propelled her into the bedroom opposite.

This was much more him! Midnight-blue walls and carpet, ceiling in the same colour, but peppered with tiny concealed lights, so that looking up from the vast double bed with its pearl-grey satin sheets would be like lying beneath the stars! And journeying to them too, if he was as good a lover as his sensuous looks suggested. Hastily pushing the thought aside, she hurried out.

'When you've quite finished nosing around,' Piers called from the living-room, 'perhaps you'll come in here and join me!'

'Righty ho!' she called in her best cockney accent.

Freshly brewed coffee awaited her, and she was sipping it when the housekeeper came in to enquire if they would be dining at home.

'Just leave out something cold for us,' Piers replied briskly. 'I'm not sure what time we'll be back.' He set down his cup and stood up. 'We'd better get cracking, Mandy. We've a lot of shopping to do, and I haven't decided where to begin. I know nothing about dressing a woman!'

Only undressing her, Amanda thought sourly, and, meeting his eyes, had the distinct impression this was precisely what he was mentally doing with her! His next words confirmed it.

'You've a lovely figure, you know, but you show it off too blatantly.'

'What's blatant about a blouse and skirt?' she asked innocently.

'That depends. In your case, green and blue satin is hardly daytime wear!'

Playfully he tweaked the ruffled collar, and as the tips of his fingers glanced against her skin she shivered with an odd sensation of excitement.

'Come on,' he said. 'Let's start with the Faubourg St Honoré. With luck, we'll get your whole wardrobe there.'

'What about the things I brought with me?' she wailed. 'I can't throw them in the street.'

'Use the dustbin!'

'What a rotten thing to say! Me clothes cost a fortune!'

'*My* clothes,' Piers said.

'I don't give a damn about *your* clothes,' she screeched, fighting back her laughter as Piers lifted his hands despairingly to his head.

'Got a pain?' she asked.

'Yes—in my neck! Now shut up!'

His glinting eyes warned her he'd had enough, but though she followed him out meekly, she was dreaming up yet more ways of taxing his patience.

Sauntering beside him down the famous shopping street, she proceeded to ooh and aah at every window displaying the most unsuitable garments, while Piers, with ill-concealed irritation, kept urging her forward. When he finally stopped, it was outside the boutique of a world-famous couturier.

'What a stuffy old place,' Amanda lied, turning up her nose at the single, exquisitely-cut dress draped in the window, and pulling Piers to a window a few yards away, where a frilly white creation was displayed. 'This is much more me!'

'It happens to be a nightgown!'

'It's too pretty to wear in bed.'

'You could take it off before you got there,' he muttered in French, and Amanda, still playing dumb, smiled innocently at him.

They finally entered an exclusive boutique further along the avenue, where she rushed instantly across to the rails, leaving Piers talking quietly to the assistant.

'Isn't this one great?' she called out, holding up a purple taffeta gown that clashed horribly with her frizzy red hair.

Piers hurried across to her, for the first time losing the *savoir faire* that had carried him through the past hours in her company.

'You must be colour-blind!' he said through clenched teeth. 'Please leave your choice of wardrobe to *me*.'

'Okay, sir,' she saluted.

'Piers,' he hissed.

'Okay, Sir Piers.'

'Just *Piers*,' he repeated in an agonised tone, and turned back to the assistant.

Demurely Amanda allowed the two of them to choose her outfits, then went to try them on. Piers' taste was for the elegant and understated. She did not dare carry them off with the aplomb they deserved, but stomped out in them, waggling her hips exaggeratedly in an effort to ruin the entire effect. That she didn't quite manage to conceal the curves of her body beneath the pliant silks and chiffons was evident from the glint in Piers' eyes.

'May I choose something for myself now?' she asked as he signalled for the clothes to be wrapped.

'Go ahead,' he said kindly.

Giving him her sweetest smile, she went to a rail and pulled out a bright red skirt from one suit, and a mauve-and-white checked jacket from another. 'Wow! This'll really knock 'em back in the King's Road!'

'But they do not belong together,' the assistant cried, horrified.

'So what?'

'They are two suits, mam'selle, not one, and would be twice as expensive.'

'Then how about this?' Amanda extracted a red-and-white striped dress.

'You'd look like an awning in it,' Piers said with a half-smile. 'Put it back and be satisfied with what you have.'

Acquiescently she did, and finally they were out in the street, with the promise that their purchases would be delivered to the apartment within the hour.

'I'd like some make-up,' Amanda said brightly, and had the satisfaction of seeing Piers wince.

'I'm sure you have more than enough.'

'But not in the latest colours.'

With a look of long suffering, he propelled her into a well-known cosmetic house, where a svelte young woman glided forward to help them.

'I'd like you to suggest a complete new range for this—er—young lady,' Piers stated.

The woman's startled glance took in Amanda's gaudy face. Then she opened a series of drawers and placed an array of jars, bottles and tubes on the counter, explaining as she went how each one was used.

'We'll take the lot,' Piers said impatiently, handing over his credit card.

'Hey, hang on!' Amanda piped up. 'Ain't you going to buy me some perfume?'

Piers gritted his teeth. 'What's your preference?'

'Something sexy.'

Piers and the beautician exchanged pained glances.
'Our scents are rather more subtle than that,' the
woman said with a forced smile, 'and for mam'selle's
personality I would suggest "Femme".'

'No, thanks. I want the one Lady Amanda uses. She
says it's the most expensive in the world, and it's got a
fantastic smell.'

'Would it be "Joy"?' the woman suggested.

'That's it!'

'At least Amanda must smell better than she looks,'
Piers muttered and nodded to the woman to add a
bottle to their purchases.

But 'Mandy' wasn't that easily satisfied. 'A little
bottle won't last me long,' she grumbled. 'Ain't you
got a bigger one?'

Happily the woman supplied it, and unhappily Piers
paid up, then marched Amanda from the shop before
she could demand anything else.

'Where are we going now?' she asked.

'Home—before you bankrupt me!'

She giggled. 'You could always marry Lady A. to
bail you out.'

'I'd sell bootlaces first!'

On reaching his apartment they found the dress
boxes already delivered, and Piers, thoroughly exhausted and looking it, flopped into the nearest
armchair. Not so Amanda; bubbling with high
spirits—for she had acquired some lovely clothes and
cosmetics—she kept up a lively commentary as she
held each garment against her and pranced round the
room.

'Can we go somewhere special tonight?' she asked
brightly. 'I'd like to show off.'

'It's been a tiring day for you.'

'I'm not the least bit tired.'

'Very well,' he sighed. 'I'll book a table somewhere
and ask Lucien to join us.'

'I thought he was annoyed with you?'

'He's probably over it by now. Anyway, he'll be curious to see what I've done with you. So mind how you behave.' He went to the door. 'I suggest you have a rest and meet me here at eight sharp.'

'All dolled up in me best bib and tucker!' she agreed, and the pained look he gave her made her vow to make it even more painful for him before the evening was over!

CHAPTER FIVE

AT a minute past eight o'clock Amanda flounced into the living-room. Piers could hardly have noticed her dress, or the 'Joy' she had drenched herself with, for his horrified attention was riveted on her bright green lids.

'*Merde!*'

Grim-faced, he caught her wrist and almost ran her to the bathroom beyond her bedroom. Grabbing her face cloth, he covered it with soap and rubbed it roughly over her face.

'I spend a fortune on cosmetics for you, and you don't damn well use them,' he grated.

'I like me old stuff better.' She tried to pull away. 'You're hurting me!'

'Be glad I'm not skinning you!'

Which he was almost doing anyway, she thought, but meekly gave in, realising she had tried his patience to the limit.

His fingers gripped her chin, bringing her face so close to his that, afraid to look into it, she shut her eyes.

'You're lovely enough without all this rubbish,' she heard him say in French. 'Pity you don't have the brains to go with it. God! Imagine going to bed with the likes of you!'

Amanda's eyes flew open, rage making them sparkle like diamonds. Not brainy enough to have an affair with, eh? she thought. Just you wait, Piers Dubray! By the time I've finished with you, you'll be on your knees begging stupid little 'Mandy' to marry you!

Startled by the thought that had come so unexpectedly into her mind, she realised what a marvellous lesson it would be for him to become so besotted by 'Mandy' that he'd beg her to become his wife. But she would have to play this fish carefully, for he was too wily to bite at ordinary bait.

Misreading her expression, he stepped back and said in English, 'Sorry I rubbed so hard.'

'So you should be.'

'Then stop looking like a clown.' He went to the door. 'Get ready again and be quick about it.'

Within five minutes Amanda rejoined him, a dab of lipstick and a hint of mascara making her look sober and demure. She could not do anything about her hair, though—not that she wanted to yet—and it glowed bright as a spring carrot!

Scrutinizing her, Piers led her down to his car. Remembering her role, Amanda feigned wide-eyed astonishment at sight of the Seine, Notre Dame, and the steep streets leading to the artists' quarters.

'Same old traffic jams as England, though,' she sniffed as they slowed to a crawl.

'This,' Piers said, ignoring her comment and waving an arm towards the crowded pavement cafés, 'is the Parisians' favourite pastime.'

'We've the same back home,' she sniffed again. 'It ain't only the French who know how to enjoy themselves.'

'I'm sure not.' He attempted no further conversation, and was still silent as he parked his car in a cobbled alley and led her into a narrow street, its predominating feature a yellow and white striped awning above the entrance to a small restaurant.

Amanda hid her disappointment, for she had been looking forward to a gourmet meal. But Piers was clearly taking no chances of bumping into any of his friends—other than Lucien, who was in on the subterfuge. But as they neared the restaurant she realised she had done Piers an injustice, for the name discreetly lettered on the façade proclaimed it to be one of the most exclusive in Paris.

Lucien was already seated at a table in the far corner of the narrow room, and he stood up as they approached, his eyes appraising. He murmured in French to Piers—Amanda couldn't hear what—who shrugged and then introduced her in English.

'Lucien, meet Mandy Jones, erstwhile personal maid to the lovely Lady Amanda!'

'Delighted.' Lucien drew Amanda's hand to his lips, then, as they took their seats, asked how she was liking Paris.

'I ain't seen much of it,' she said brightly. 'We were too busy shopping.'

'Shame on you, Piers,' his friend chided. 'You should at least have taken Mandy to the Crillon for lunch.'

'Clothes were our top priority,' came the reply. 'I spent a small fortune on her.'

'I never asked you to spend no money on me,' Amanda said indignantly.

'*Any* money.'

'Money's money,' she snapped. 'And I don't want your friend thinking I'm a gold-digger.'

'He wouldn't be far off the mark. You drove a hard bargain for playing this part.'

'You didn't have to accept it.'

'What about a drink?' Lucien interjected tactfully. 'Champagne, Mandy?'

'Ooh yes. I love them bubbles!'

Piers raised an eyebrow, but Lucien's smile was kind as he gave their order to the waiter. Then the two men lapsed into French, leaving Amanda to sit and fidget, feigning boredom. What a pity she hadn't said she'd been an au pair in France, then she could have joined in the conversation!

And what an interesting conversation it was, ranging over the political situation in Europe, a forthcoming election in South America, and the current state of the stock market.

She gathered the last was Lucien's profession, and, from the way he referred to 'our branch office in Rio . . . our parent company in New York . . .' guessed him to be a well-heeled young man. But then, she couldn't imagine Piers having someone poor as a close friend. When all was said and done, to make money one had to go where the money was.

Cogitating on this, she was surprised he hadn't jumped at the chance of marrying Amanda Herbert—regardless of her looks. Unless, of course, he was conceited enough to believe he could have both money *and* beauty.

Her eyes rested on him. He was certainly handsome enough to take his pick among the current crop of heiresses! Indeed, if she hadn't overheard him in the shrubbery yesterday she would have fallen for him herself. Irritated that she should be thinking this way, she scowled, and Lucien, noticing, instantly reverted to English.

'Please forgive us. We're very rude to be talking in French.'

'Gentlemen are often rude,' she said sarcastically. 'They think it's their right!'

He coloured with embarrassment, but Piers chuckled. 'I should have warned you about Mandy's tongue, old chap. It's sharper than her wits!'

'And you're better-looking than your manners,' she came back at him.

'Hey, you two,' Lucien pacified, 'you're meant to be engaged, not at war!'

'Lucien's right,' Piers agreed. 'Stop provoking me, Mandy.'

'You're the one who's provoking,' Lucien said to him in French. 'You sit there ignoring the poor girl, then wonder why she's bad-tempered.'

Amanda coughed into her hand to hide a chuckle,

and knew that if Piers had his friend's good nature this whole charade would never have been necessary. They might even have made two families happy by falling in love! Of course, there was no knowing the staying power of a man with such a rakish reputation, and she would always have wondered if his feelings for her were coloured by her inheritance!

'Time we ate,' Lucien broke into her thoughts. 'You must be hungry.'

'Starving,' she agreed, giving Piers an accusatory glance.

'What a nag you are,' he muttered. 'Pity I ever started this whole damn thing!'

Amanda scraped back her chair. 'Okay. Give me my money and——'

'Stop threatening me,' he hissed. 'We struck a bargain, and unless you keep to it you won't get a cent from me. Is that clear?'

'Yes, sir. But if you can't be civil to me, I——'

'Shut up,' he snapped, 'and decide what you want to eat!'

'Would you like me to help you choose?' Lucien intervened.

She nodded, and he placed his menu in front of her and leaned close as he explained the various specialities.

Amanda was surprised by the length and thickness of his lashes, which were several shades darker than his blond hair, and decided he was quite a dishy specimen in his own right. If she weren't determined to give Piers his comeuppance, she'd have enjoyed getting to know Lucien better. Conscious of Piers watching them, an imp of mischief made her moisten her lips with the tip of her tongue and give Lucien her most delectable smile.

His eyes flickered and for a brief instant he was motionless, then he straightened away from her.

'What the hell's got into you?' Piers asked him

irritably in French. 'You're staring at the girl as if you've never seen one before.'

'With such potential, no.'

'Well, keep away until I've finished with her! Then she's all yours!'

Amanda's blood boiled. Did he but know it, Piers was digging his grave deeper by the minute! Well, she would show him! Turning to Lucien, she flashed him another smile, and once again his eyes flickered.

'Want me to translate more of the menu for you,' he asked, 'or have you made up your mind?'

'I think I'll have a hamburger and chips.'

His mouth fell open. 'I—er—I'm afraid you won't be able to get that here.'

'Blimey! It ain't much of a restaurant, is it? In England you can get hamburger and chips anywhere. Why don't we leave and go to a Mcdonalds?'

Piers looked ready to burst a blood vessel, and Lucien said hastily, 'This is one of the best restaurants in Paris, Mandy, and I'm sure you'll love the food once you taste it. Why not let me choose something for you?'

This turned out to be lightly sautéed goose liver, served on a purée of sorrel, followed by lamb cutlets in flaky pastry. Piers, ignoring them, settled for melon and steak, then—after carefully conferring with the wine waiter—he chose a 1970 Château Margaux.

Awaiting her opportunity to rile him again, Amanda knew it had come as a glass of the magnificent ruby red wine was poured for her. Taking a sip, she gave a dramatic shudder.

'Ugh! It's horrible! I'll have a Coke.'

'You'll have the wine,' Piers rasped.

'No, I won't. It tastes like vinegar.'

'Only because your palate's uneducated. A glass of wine with your meals is part of your job. Mother will expect it of you.'

'Then she'd better expect me to be sick!'

Lucien couldn't restrain a laugh but Piers, too incensed to find anything funny in it, turned his head away in disgust.

'How long will we be staying with your mother?' Amanda went on.

'I've told you. Long enough to convince her I've no intention of marrying Amanda.'

'You think you'll convince her you want to marry *me*?' Amanda giggled. 'I ain't no lady, and all the smart clothes in the world won't make me one.'

'Who says you aren't a lady?' Lucien interposed. 'You happen to be a very lovely one.'

'Your friend don't agree.'

'*Doesn't*,' Piers snarled.

'That's what I said,' she retorted, feigning surprise. 'You *don't*.'

'You've met your match with this one, Piers,' Lucien chuckled.

'Very funny,' Piers muttered gloomily. 'This whole débâcle is beginning to get on my nerves.'

'Let's call it a day, then,' Amanda said. 'I already told you I'm willing to pack it in.'

'And I told you we have to go through with it.' He glared at her. 'The best thing is to keep your mouth shut in front of my mother.'

'Like me to use sign language?' Amanda asked, and was sorry Piers' retort was cut short by the arrival of the cheeseboard.

As he gave his attention to it, Lucien caught Amanda's eye, and leaned towards her.

'Don't mind Piers' bad temper,' he murmured. 'He's had a tough time lately.'

'How come?'

'Overwork. Three years' non-stop commuting between California and France is beginning to get to him.'

So Piers *did* work hard! She would have liked to question Lucien more, and vowed to do so at the first opportunity.

'At least she's got decent table manners,' Piers commented to him in French. 'Probably picked up a few pointers from the Herberts.'

'Most people have passable table manners these days,' Lucien replied.

'This girl isn't "most people". She's a one off! You should have seen how she wanted to come out with me tonight.'

'You were the one who chose her,' Lucien reminded him. 'There were plenty of others you could have asked. Mariette, for one. She'd have jumped at the chance.'

'And then stuck to me like a leech. At least I won't have trouble getting rid of this one!'

You can say that again, Amanda thought mutinously. Once I have you eating out of my hand, you won't see me for dust! A gleam came into her eye, and, lifting her wine glass, she crooked her little finger exaggeratedly.

'Don't do that,' Piers burst out.

'Do what?'

'Curl your finger! Put it back with the rest of them!'

'Like this, Mandy,' Lucien explained, and curved all his fingers around the stem of his glass.

'You're very kind to help me,' she said.

Surprisingly, colour seeped into his face, and she began to suspect she was having more of an impact on him than she had realised. But then, she was a foreigner to him, and he probably found her speech quaint. Piers didn't, for sure. But then he was a sharper, tougher man. She threw Lucien another smile. She had never gone for blond men, but there was something about this one . . .

Beneath her lashes, her eyes slid from him to Piers. They were like chalk and cheese, and once again she couldn't fathom how they came to be friends. Maybe it was because they were opposites. On the other hand, they might have more in common than met the eye, which meant Piers was either kinder than he let on, or Lucien tougher!

'Getting to like the wine?' Piers asked her suddenly.
'It needs more sugar.'

He choked on his mouthful and when he spoke again his voice was taut with the effort to keep control of himself. 'Claret is never sweet. Red wine rarely is.'

'Then I'll stick with white if that's okay with you?'

'Perfectly. We produce white in our own vineyards, so you'll at least be pleasing my mother.'

'Stop being so hard on the girl,' Lucien warned in French. 'She's doing her best.'

'That's what scares me,' Piers replied, also in his own tongue. 'Mother's going to wonder what I see in this idiot I'm supposed to love!'

'She knows you're a pushover for a pretty face, and this one's exceptionally lovely. So stop looking at the poor kid as if you want to strangle her!'

'You're right,' Piers sighed. 'Otherwise I'll be a few thousand pounds down the drain.'

Amanda, on her last mouthful, almost laughed aloud. The longer this little playlet continued, the more hilarious she was finding it, and the more she looked forward to the finale.

'What's for pud?' she demanded. 'Any chance of a treacle tart?'

'Not here, I'm afraid. But why not try crêpes Suzette? They're pancakes with a special Grand Marnier sauce.'

'Gran what?'

'Orange liqueur,' Lucien explained, just managing to hide a grin.

'Sounds great,' she giggled. 'I like oranges.'

This time he could not restrain a laugh, and, still smiling, he ordered the crêpes for them both, though Piers settled for coffee and brandy, which he sipped sullenly.

Silence fell on the three of them, and Amanda watched Piers from beneath her lashes. The golden glow of the room made his skin appear a darker bronze, his hair even blacker, reminding her that, though they were distantly related, he was foreign, with the passion of a Latin—for anger as well as love. Not that love figured much in his life. According to him, he was only interested in passion. She tried picturing him as a lover, and was disconcerted to realise that she didn't have to try too hard. He'd be demanding, tempestuous and utterly experienced, knowing how to take pleasure as well as give it.

It was after midnight when they finally emerged from the restaurant, and Amanda, with the strain of playing 'Mandy' all day beginning to tell on her, swayed slightly as the fresh air hit her.

'Wine gone to your head?' Piers questioned.

'No. Just tired.'

Unexpectedly he put a hand beneath her elbow as he guided her to his car and helped her in.

Lucien bent down, the better to see Amanda's face. 'Good luck, Mandy, and don't be scared of meeting Madame Dubray. You'll find her easier to get on with than her son!'

'Anyone would be easier to get on with than him!' she said pertly, and Lucien chuckled.

'Come down for the weekend,' Piers suggested.

'I might at that. If only to give Mandy moral support!'

'I'm the one who'll be needing support!' Piers' look was wry as he slid his long frame behind the wheel.

'Am I really so impossible?' Amanda asked as they turned into the brightly-lit boulevard.

'Only a little more than most women,' he grunted.

'You don't like my sex?'

'Only in bed. For the rest, I can't fathom them. Nor do I have any wish to.'

'What about when you marry? If you don't get to

know your wife you won't have much of a relationship with her.'

'That's a pretty profound statement, coming from you,' he said.

'I heard it on the telly,' she retorted. 'Telly teaches you a lot.'

'I'll take your word for it.' He slowed at an intersection, then gathered speed again.

'How was I tonight?' she asked, to change the subject.

'Not bad.' He paused. 'Though I can't say the same for myself. I was rude to you, and I apologise.' Abruptly he lifted her hand and planted a kiss on it.

It was the second time her hand had been kissed today, but whereas she had quickly forgotten the touch of Lucien's lips, the pressure of Piers' mouth lingered. Watch it! she warned herself. It might be fun getting him to fall for 'Mandy', but it would be disastrous if *she* fell for him!

'What if your mother doesn't like me?' she questioned, anxious to steer clear of her thoughts.

'I assure you she will. She's no ogre, and is probably as nervous of meeting *you* as you are of her.'

'What have you told her about me?'

'That you're unspoilt, unsophisticated, and utterly delectable.'

Amanda grinned. 'Men always say that about the girls they want to marry!'

'I've never been in that situation, so I wouldn't know.'

'Me neither. I've been too busy with boy friends.'

'I'm sure they've wanted to bother with *you*,' he replied, drawing the car to a stop in the courtyard of his apartment block.

Shrugging, she jumped out, finding his proximity stifling.

It was the same in the elevator, and she stood as far away from him as possible. The slight smile playing at the corners of his mouth told her he was aware of it, and the instant he opened his front door she slipped past him with a murmured 'Good night'.

'Not so fast,' he said, and with a swift movement pulled her into his arms and planted a kiss full on her mouth.

Amanda's first instinct was to draw away, but the caressing movement of his lips was her undoing, and her own parted. Instantly his tongue slipped between them, gently exploring the soft interior before sliding along the side of her own tongue. She trembled and responded, and he pressed her more tightly against the length of his body, his hands snaking round her hips to draw the fullness of her breasts and the flatness of her stomach close to his own body, so that she felt the hard swell of his arousal.

For one tantalising moment she knew an insane desire to give in to him, and even as she fought it he won his own battle and pushed her away.

'It wouldn't do, I'm afraid,' he said thickly. 'You're the one complication I don't need in my life!'

'Chance would be a fine thing!' she snapped, grabbing at her tattered pride.

'It wouldn't be chance with you, Mandy. It would be a certainty!'

'Bastard!'

He laughed. 'I hope you don't sleepwalk, because I'm locking my door!'

Fuming, she stalked away, but once in her room she calmed down and let her thoughts stray. The direction they took didn't please her, for she was piercingly aware of Piers' presence across the corridor where—her imagination running riot—she pictured him in bed, nude for certain, his sinewy body as bronzed as his face.

Hour after hour she tossed and turned restlessly, and though she tried to deny the cause, she finally had to concede that she ached for the sight and touch of him, for his virile body and the enveloping strength of his arms.

It must be the wine, she told herself, padding into the bathroom for a glass of water. She had met many physically desirable men, but none had affected her like this. What was it about the dratted man? Or was she simply ripe for a love affair?

She stared at her reflection in the mirror, seeing the excited glow in her eyes, the pointed nipples through her filmy nightgown. Yes, that was it. She was experiencing a normal woman's desire for sex; a need to touch and be touched. And Piers merely happened to be available.

On this comforting note she returned to bed, resolutely refusing to admit that her need for him might conceivably not be as simple as she would have herself believe.

CHAPTER SIX

THE tattered postcard of Château Charmaine that had sat at the back of Amanda's dressing table drawer for as long as she could remember hadn't prepared her for the magnificent stone edifice which met her eyes as Piers' Maserati turned the final corner of the winding, tree-lined drive and drew up outside it. Though she had always considered her own home beautiful, it could not compare with the loveliness of this fairy-tale castle with its graceful turrets and mullioned windows. No wonder Piers was so lukewarm about inheriting Herbert House!

'Don't be nervous,' he said, misinterpreting her silence. 'Do as I say and everything will be fine.'

Amanda nodded as she climbed out of the car, and silently they crunched across the gravel to the stone steps leading up to the massive oaken door.

An elderly, hawk-nosed manservant—'Michel's been with us as long as I can remember,' Piers murmured swiftly to her—pulled it open and greeted him with a smile that crinkled his eyes and criss-crossed his face into a myriad lines.

One mark in Piers' favour, Amanda thought approvingly, noting it, and heard Michel say that Madame Dubray would be down shortly, and he had instructions to escort mam'selle to her suite.

'I'll do it,' Piers smiled, and propelled Amanda across the vast hall, its flagstoned floor warmed by rugs, its walls lined with tapestries.

At the top of the stairs the corridor branched left and right, and Piers led her along the west wing and into a suite with a view of the formal garden.

'I think you'll find everything you need here,' he

said, as she pretended to be astonished at the opulence of gilded furniture, thick carpet and glittering lamps.

'What me mum wouldn't give to have a house like this!' she burbled, bouncing exuberantly from the bedroom to the bathroom. 'Blimey! A sunken bath! You mean they had 'em in the olden days?'

'I had this installed several years ago,' he said acidly.

'Must have cost you a bomb. Where'd you find the money?'

'You have a misguided picture of me, Mandy. Contrary to what you think, I work damned hard—and successfully too.'

'But you wouldn't say no to a rich wife, would you?'

'Nor would most men!'

'Then how come you turned down Lady Amanda?'

'If I remember rightly, you said she was all set to turn *me* down!'

'She might have changed her mind when she saw you close up,' Amanda leered.

'I suggest we stop discussing Lady Amanda,' he said smoothly, 'and concentrate on persuading my mother that I'm in love with *you*.'

'I'll do me best.' Amanda did a little jig around the room. 'Fancy me in a real French château! I wish everyone at Herbert House could see me.'

'Forget Herbert House. You're my fiancée now.' The very idea seemed impossible to him, and he shook his head.

'What's wrong?' she asked with pretended innocence.

'Nothing, yet. But when I think what I've let myself in for ...' He sighed. 'I figured you'd be easy to mould, but you're about as malleable as a rock!'

'Don't you think our subterage will work then?'

'Subterfuge,' he corrected, 'and it *has* to work.' He went to the door. 'I'd better go and prepare my mother for you.'

'You make me sound like an operation.'

'A massive one! I only wish I didn't have to fool her.' He sighed, then seemed to push the thought away. 'I'll see you in the sitting-room—it's next to the library—in about a quarter of an hour.'

'Shall I change?'

'No need.'

She glanced down at herself. 'Don't s'pose it makes much difference anyway. One stuffy outfit's as boring as another.'

'Ungrateful wretch!'

Amanda grinned as the door shut behind him, then went to the mirror to touch up her face—but with a lighter hand this time. She wondered if Madame Dubray would recognise her—women were generally more perceptive than men—then decided probably not. After all, it was years since they had met. She frowned at her reflection, suddenly disliking the subterfuge as much as Piers, and wishing, for the first time, that she hadn't entered into it.

A light tap at the door made her swing round, and she opened it to be confronted by a middle-aged woman with soft white hair and intense dark eyes that looked at her with a directness that put her on guard. This must be Piers' mother. She was tiny, but high heels and an elaborate, up-swept coiffure gave her an illusion of stateliness, matched by a gracious manner.

'You must be Mandy,' she said in charmingly accented English.

'Yes.' Amanda warmed instantly to the face she recalled dimly from her childhood. 'And you're——' she hesitated, 'you must be Piers' mum.'

'That's right. We're meant to be meeting officially in a little while, but I thought it would be nice to have a chat first.'

Amanda stepped aside, and Madame Dubray came in and sat in an armchair, while Amanda perched on the dressing table stool.

'I was quite surprised when Piers called me the other day and said he was engaged. He hadn't spoken of you before and I—I didn't realise he was serious about anyone.'

'It was all pretty sudden.' Amanda felt some explanation was due, but carefully said little in case it conflicted with Piers' version. 'You know what men are like! They hate being caught!'

'Well, you've undoubtedly caught my son.' The dark eyes crinkled humorously. 'I've never heard him speak of any girl in such loving terms.'

'Honest? What did he say?'

'That you're beautiful, unspoiled, have a lively sense of humour—and that he loves you.' Madame Dubray's hands tapped a nervous tattoo on the arm of her chair. 'Now I've met you, I can see why he does. You're very pretty.'

There was a pause, and Amanda was beset by such an attack of conscience at fooling this charming woman that she was on the point of confessing the truth when Madame Dubray spoke again.

'Piers says you've lost both parents and have no living relatives.'

Oh, he had, had he? Remembering the trouble she'd taken to invent an abandoned mum left to bring up three fatherless children, a stepfather who'd beaten them, and an aged granny in a wheelchair, Amanda's good intentions vanished under an upsurge of temper. So a poor, hard-working family wasn't good enough for Piers Snooty Dubray. Well, she'd make him pay for that!

'I'm sorry if I've been tactless,' her hostess murmured, seeing Amanda frown.

'You haven't—truly. I'm used to being an orphan.' She puffed up her hair. 'I know you ain't happy Piers chose me—I'm not daft, you know—but I'll do me best to make him a good wife.'

'I'm sure you will. I understand you were brought up in the country and worked in a—in a house.'

'I was a parlour-maid. No need beating about the bush. I'm not ashamed of it.'

'Why should you be? Honest work is always something to be proud of.' The dark eyes twinkled. 'It might amuse you to know that Piers' great-great-grandfather was a pedlar.'

'How did he come up in the world?'

'By running off with the daughter of a wealthy landowner!'

Amanda laughed. 'I bet you're sorry Piers isn't doing the same! If anyone's loaded, it's Lady A.'

'You know about her?'

'Yes. I——' Suddenly realising that Piers hadn't told his mother 'Mandy' had worked for the Herbert family, she changed her tactics. 'He mentioned her the other day. Said you were pretty keen on the match.'

'I was. But that's all in the past now. You're the girl he loves and I'm happy to welcome you.'

'You're very kind to me,' Amanda said sincerely.

'I'd be foolish if I weren't.'

Amanda gave Madame Dubray full marks for her intelligent ability to accept a situation that must dismay her. There was no doubt that she did not approve of her son's choice of a wife, but she was astute enough to know that antagonising either of them could lead to an estrangement. She wondered what her own parents would do in similar circumstances, and doubted whether her mother could be as forbearing.

'Well, I'm glad we get on okay,' she said aloud. 'I hope I won't shame you.'

'Of course you won't! Don't even think it. Be your natural self, my dear, and you'll soon learn the ropes.'

'If I don't trip over 'em first!'

Madame Dubray chuckled and went to the door. 'I'd better go and see Piers or he'll be wondering where I am.'

'Will you tell him we've met?'

'Naturally. My son and I have no secrets from each other.'

That's what *you* think, Amanda thought ironically, and saw him getting a box on the ear from his mama in the not too distant future!

Alone again, Amanda sank on to the bed. Now she had met Madame Dubray, she had lost what little respect she had for Piers. With such an understanding mother, he should have had the guts to say categorically that he wouldn't marry a girl he didn't love. Indeed, the more she thought about it, the more incredible it was that he had resorted to this nonsensical charade.

Getting slowly to her feet, she gave a final pat to her bird's nest hair, and went downstairs.

In the hall she hesitated, not certain which massive door opened into the sitting-room. She tapped on the nearest one, and, getting no reply, walked in to find herself in the library.

With a few minutes to spare, she decided to spend them at her favourite pastime—book-browsing. Picking one out at random, and discovering it to be a French version of Keats, one of her favourite poets, she curled up with it on a window-seat, half-concealed by a heavy velvet curtain.

'*Thou still unravished bride of quietness, Thou foster-child of silence and slow time . . .*'

So immersed was she in the lovely words, she was unaware of two people entering. Only when she heard Madame Dubray's voice did she realise her own embarrassing position, for the woman spoke in English, and what she said made it impossible for Amanda to reveal herself.

'She's a lovely-looking girl, Piers, I grant you that, but she'll bore you to death within a year.'

'That's where you're wrong,' he answered in French. 'She's as bright as she's beautiful, and she has an unusual sense of humour. This isn't a whim, Maman. I've been keen on her for a long while.'

'Pity you forgot to mention it! If you had, I wouldn't have insisted you should meet Amanda.' There was the creak of a chair. 'Was she really as dreadful as you said on the phone?'

'A walking nightmare.'

Amanda stifled her laughter as Piers launched into a description of the apparition at the window, and she was more and more astounded that he had been taken in by it. But then, he'd expected the worst!

'Poor child, to be so plain,' Madame Dubray commiserated.

'And so lacking in charm,' her son added. 'Some plain women can be very attractive, but *that* one . . .'

'Ah, well,' his mother sighed, the expression signifying the death of her hopes, 'but I still think Mandy's wrong for you. She'll be out of depth in your lifestyle and could end up extremely unhappy.'

A lengthy silence ensued, and Amanda was certain guilt was tying Piers' tongue. And so it should! Now his mother had accepted that he was not going to marry the girl of her choice, he should come clean. Even as she prayed he would—for then so would she— he spoke.

'Let's get one thing clear, Maman. I love Mandy and I intend to marry her. So let's drop the subject, shall we, and go to meet her?'

A moment later the library was silent, and Amanda stepped from her hiding-place, so incensed by Piers' cowardice that she was more determined than ever to get back at him.

Hurriedly she returned to her room and re-appraised her appearance. She looked far too ladylike in her new clothes, and since the 'Mandy' ones she had brought with her to France had been consigned to the refuse bin she had to make the worst of what she had!

Unbuttoning her red blouse to the waist, she clinched it with a wide green belt from another dress. Then, taking her nail-scissors, she slit the side of her skirt almost to the thigh. That should make Piers' eyes pop for a start!

Next her hair. Piling the front as high as it would go, she held it in position with a red ribbon which she took from the collar of a blouse. There—that made her look like a waitress in a topless bar! Turning from the mirror, she spotted the large bottle of 'Joy' he had brought her. Removing the stopper, she gave a quick squirt behind the ears. Mmm—heavenly! Another squirt, then another—not quite so heavenly now! A few more squirts and she nearly knocked herself out!

Satisfied at last, she ran downstairs.

The thunderous look Piers gave her as she sauntered into the sitting-room affected her not one bit, though the wrinkling of Madame Dubray's nose did, which made her decide to tone down her manner to compensate for her toned-up appearance.

'Hope I ain't late?' she enquired of the room at large.

'Not at all,' her hostess said kindly. 'Would you like some coffee, Mandy? Or do you prefer tea?'

'Coffee's great, thanks.'

As Piers came across to her with it, he gave a violent sneeze and nearly dropped the cup. A bland expression on her face, Amanda watched as he put a handkerchief to his nose.

'What the hell have you done?' he whispered. 'Poured the whole damned perfume bottle on your head?'

'Did I put on too much, then?' she asked innocently. 'It smells so fantastic I just went on squirting.'

With a strangled sound, he strode to the windows and flung them wide, taking in several deep breaths.

'I'm ever so sorry,' Amanda apologised to her hostess. 'Is it making you feel sick too?'

'Well, it's somewhat overpowering. Perfume should

be used subtly, my dear—just a hint to make one think it's the scent of your skin.'

'I'll remember next time.' Amanda glanced at Piers. 'Want me to go wash it off?'

'Later,' he said curtly. 'And put on something decent at the same time.'

'Piers!' his mother scolded. 'Don't be so rude.'

'What I meant,' he said hastily, 'is that Mandy's lovely enough without getting herself up like a—up like a——' Words failed him, and he lapsed into silence.

Madame Dubray studied Amanda carefully. 'You weren't quite so—er—startling when I saw you in your room, so I can only assume you're trying to make some point to my son.'

'Got it right first go!' For the second time Amanda applauded the woman's perspicacity. 'It's time he learned that nagging me is the best way of making me do the opposite!'

'Hear that, Piers?'

'Loud and clear, Maman.' He stalked across to a chair, temper tightening his mouth. 'Maybe I'll leave *you* to groom Mandy.'

His mother threw her a humorous glance, and once more Amanda wished she could be herself. Sighing inwardly, she reached for a cream cake.

'How nice meeting someone who isn't on a diet,' her hostess commented.

'I'm lucky. Riding and swimming have always kept me——' She stopped—too late—for Piers gave a laugh.

'Riding and swimming? How did you manage to fit them in between the polishing and dusting?'

'Quite easily. Why else do you think I worked in the country?'

'We've a pool here if you like swimming,' Madame Dubray interjected hastily, 'but no stable, I'm afraid. Piers was thrown as a child, and hasn't felt the same towards horses since.'

'He should have got straight back on when he fell off,' Amanda stated.

'Difficult with a broken leg,' Piers said silkily, and Amanda conceded him the last word.

'I've been meaning to tell you, dear,' his mother reminded herself, 'I'm giving a small dinner-party tomorrow evening to introduce Mandy to a few of our friends.'

The statement acted on Piers like a bullet, for he jumped up so fast that he sent the small table beside him crashing.

'What on earth for? I mean, I—I wanted her to settle down first—get used to things . . .'

'You talk like I'm some kind of freak,' Amanda grumbled.

As he began to reply, Michel came in to say he was wanted on the telephone. Hurrying out, he gave Amanda a warning look that told her to mind her tongue in his absence. Not that she needed reminding, for she had no intention of distressing Madame Dubray any further. Demurely she went on eating her cake and sipping her coffee.

'You have lovely hair,' he hostess commented. 'It's such an unusual colour.'

'It's too red,' Amanda said, delighted she could be honest about something. 'Think I should tone it down?'

'It might be an idea. Though perhaps, if you softened the style, the colour wouldn't be quite so—er—startling.'

Amanda nodded, wishing she could revert to her true self entirely, and imagining Piers' reaction when she finally did. Would he be furious at the joke she had played on him, or amused? Both, probably, though she hoped amusement would predominate, for then they could be friends.

Only friends? She shied away from the question,

realising that her stay here would be traumatic enough without her adding to it by thinking of the future.

Better to leave that in the lap of the gods—provided she could depend on the gods being on her side!

CHAPTER SEVEN

It was no flamboyant Mandy, but a very ladylike one who sailed into the drawing-room next evening—the skirt of her cream silk organza floating around her—to meet the dozen or so guests gathered to scrutinise the girl who had finally managed to ensnare Piers Dubray.

Earlier that evening her hostess had come to Amanda's room to advise her on what to wear, doing so with her usual tact.

'Please don't think I'm interfering, my dear, but you did say you'd like my help in choosing something suitable.'

'And I meant it.' Amanda opened the door of her walk-in cupboard, and in no time a dress was selected.

'You have lovely clothes,' Madame Dubray murmured.

'Piers bought them for me. He's got very definite ideas about the way I should look.'

'Because he wants you to do justice to yourself.' Dark eyes surveyed Amanda. 'If you don't mind my saying so, I think a softer hairstyle would suit you even more than the one you have now. Why not let Henriette—my personal maid—see what she can suggest? She has magic hands.'

'As long as she doesn't come near me with the scissors!'

'No fear of that. And if you don't like what she does, you can always change it back again.'

'Righty ho!' Amanda said cheerily. 'And thanks for being such a sweetie.'

She was thinking of this as she glided across the salon with the eyes of every guest riveted on her.

Piers stepped smartly forward to take her arm, and

she hid a grin at his feigned besotted expression. Maybe she'd go easy on him this evening? After all, she didn't want to give him an ulcer!

'Quite a stunning picture,' he whispered. 'I hope you'll behave as well as you look!'

Trust him to give her a backhanded compliment! For *that* she'd intensify his misery! Pulling him over to the drinks table, where a white-jacketed steward was dispensing champagne, she called out at the top of her voice, 'Anyone for booze?'

Piers went stiff as an icicle, then managed a strangled laugh. 'Mandy and her little jokes!'

With fingers of steel he propelled her round the room to introduce her to the guests—though the speed with which he did made it patently obvious that he was unwilling to allow her more than a brief 'hello' to anyone.

When he finally deposited her in a chair, well away from everyone else, she awarded him full marks for his neat handling of what could have been an embarrassing situation for him. But he needn't think he was going to get away with it so easily. Her worst was yet to come!

Several more guests arrived, and as Madame Dubray went to greet them Piers half-rose to do the same, then, thinking better of it, remained glued to her side. Determined to foil him, Amanda sat forward on her chair, then, before he could stop her, darted across to the buffet where several people were helping themselves to the delicious assortment of canapés.

'May I get you something, mam'selle?' a jovial, red-faced man asked her in heavily-accented English.

Amanda pointed to a crystal bowl of glistening Beluga caviar, every grain separate, black and perfect. 'What's those funny antlike things?'

The man's face grew redder. '*Mon Dieu!* That's caviar.' With a silver teaspoon he placed a dollop on a plate, added a slice of toasted brioche, kept warm in a napkin, and handed it to her.

With a high giggle, she dug her forefinger into the caviar and scooped some into her mouth. 'Ugh! It tastes like fish paste!'

Heavy breathing in her ear told her that Piers was beside her, and she turned and waggled her fishy finger at him. 'Hullo, luv, want a lick?'

'Only if it includes your hand,' he said suavely, then gave her red-faced companion a strained smile. 'Mademoiselle Mandy's a real tease, Louis. You mustn't take her seriously.'

With a wary glance at her, Louis backed away, and Piers, a smile pasted on his face, took the plate from her. 'Care for something else, my dearest?'

'Such as?'

'Strangulation?'

She gave a ripple of laughter, forgetting to make it Mandy's high-pitched one. Noticing the melodious sound, Piers' eyes narrowed, and Amanda, furious with herself, diverted his attention by giving him a little push and exclaiming, 'Well, look who's here. Lucien!'

Genuinely delighted at the sight of a sympathetic face, she darted across the room to him. 'Thank goodness you've come! I've never met so many stuffy people. They should be mounted on a wall!'

'And you should be painted and framed,' Lucien said admiringly.

'It must be the new hairstyle. Glad you like it.'

Henriette, after one look at it earlier on, had instantly guessed the bright colour came from a bottle, and had offered to wash it out. Knowing the one thing she daren't do was let her hair revert to its natural auburn glory, Amanda had refused, and the surprised woman had contented herself with brushing it into a smooth coil and pinning it firmly to the top of her head.

Worried that such a sophisticated look might not go with her flashy personality, she had teased the sides into frizzy curls the instant Henriette had left, making the style more reminiscent of Nell Gwynne. And since that good lady had managed to bring a king to his knees, surely 'Mandy' stood a chance of bringing an arrogant Frenchman to his?

But she was careful to hide these thoughts as Lucien led her gallantly to a small settee. 'I didn't expect you down till the weekend,' she said.

'Nor did Piers, from the way he's glowering at me!'

She tossed her head. 'He's a right pain in the neck. Beats me how you can be friends with such a snob.'

'The one thing Piers isn't is a snob.'

'Then why is he so horrible to me?'

'Nerves, I think. He doesn't like deceiving his mother.'

'Then let him tell her the truth.'

'I wish he would. But now he's got himself into this situation, he's determined to see it through to the bitter end.'

'With me being the bitter end, I s'pose?'

Lucien chuckled. 'Personally, I think you're the sweetest!'

'You're flirting with me.'

'Do you mind?'

Amanda studied him. In stylish dinner jacket and frilled white shirt, he appeared the typical, well-heeled man-about-town. Yet the warmth and compassion he exuded told her he was no hedonistic playboy.

'You're taking your time answering,' he teased.

'Because I'm trying to make you out.'

'Don't. Accept me as your friend and see what happens.'

She had a pretty good idea what would happen when he finally learned her identity, and wished the thought could excite her. Yet, despite his blond good looks, he left her cold—unlike a certain black-haired Adonis with blue eyes. She stopped, aghast. The last thing she wanted was to fall for a womanising, bad-tempered lecher!'

'Why the scowl?' Lucien asked.

'Just thinking of the future.'

'It should be a wonderful one for you.'

'Three thousand pounds won't go all that far.'

'Three thou——!'

'That's what Piers is paying me for this little job. I've been wondering what to do with it.' She genuinely didn't know what a 'Mandy' type *would* do.

'Invest it,' Lucien said.

'Too boring. I'd rather buy some sexy clothes and go on a cruise. That's the best way of catching a rich husband!' Seeing him raise an eyebrow, she feigned surprise. 'Can't see me getting one?'

'On the contrary. I think you can get any man you want. There's a quality about you that ...' He frowned. 'When you and Piers call it a day, I'd like to get to know you better, so promise you won't disappear into the blue!'

'I ain't zooming off to the moon!'

'I was hoping you'd stay in Paris.'

'Why? I'm no good-time girl, if that's what you think.'

His sherry-gold eyes twinkled. 'I think you're a very sweet young lady who isn't half as belligerent as she makes out.'

Amanda was glad Piers wasn't as perceptive. But then, someone so self-centred was blind to everyone else. Come to think of it, Piers didn't have a single redeeming feature, characterwise. Glancing over Lucien's shoulder, she saw him talking to a thin blonde girl, and was forced to concede that on the physical side it was quite another matter. There, he had everything going for him! Yet a meaningful relationship couldn't be sustained by the physical side alone. There had to be something more. Damn! She was doing it again: regarding Piers as a potential husband! The whole thing was crazy!

'Hey there,' Lucien tapped her arm. 'You've gone miles away.'

'No, I haven't,' she lied. 'I'm thinking over what you said.'

'Good. And there's one more thing for you to think over. If you'd care to work in Paris, I'll find you a job. Just let me know what your preference is—modelling—secretarial, whatever—and I'll contact some of my friends.'

Playing her part to the full, she gave him a bold stare. 'Underneath that kind offer, I still think your aim is to get me into bed!'

'Not that incomprehensible, surely? I'm a normal man and you're an exceptionally beautiful girl. But my offer to help you is genuine. You're not only decorative, Mandy, you're bright enough to get any place you want.'

If only Piers was saying this, Amanda thought moodily, and bit back a sigh.

'All I want,' she said aloud, 'is to be the sort of girl Piers would marry.'

Lucien stiffened. 'You mean you've fallen for him?'

'Don't be daft! I just fancy the life he leads. Maybe if I learned how to mind me p's and q's, I'd get a ring out of him.'

Lucien opened his mouth, then shut it again, and watching the varying expressions flit across his face, she knew it wouldn't take much to get a ring from *him*. At the moment, only her gaucherie held him back, though she was convinced he subconsciously sensed she was not all she seemed. She suspected Madame Dubray sensed it too. Only Piers, intent on pulling the wool over his mother's eyes, had pulled it well and truly over his own!

'Let's forget the future,' she shrugged. 'At the moment I'm Piers' fiancée.'

Before Lucien could comment, Michel opened the double doors and announced that dinner was served.

From the corner of her eye Amanda saw Piers move away from the insipid-looking blonde and stride towards her.

'Hi,' Lucien greeted him. 'Hope you don't mind my coming down uninvited?'

'I rather assumed you would!' Bright blue eyes raked Amanda. 'Looks an angel, doesn't she? Until she opens her mouth and spoils it!'

'I could say the same about you,' she flared.

'You mean you see me as an angel? I'm flattered.'

'Don't be. Lucifer's got a limited future!'

Piers was so taken aback by her retort that Lucien burst out laughing. 'Mandy wins that round, my friend. Concede defeat and take her in to dinner.'

'Unless you'd prefer to escort Miss Flat Chest,' Amanda suggested sweetly.

'Jealous?' came the mocking question.

'Disappointed. We're here to convince your mother we're a pair of love birds, yet you spend your time ogling a pair of non-existent boobs!'

Piers' eyes lowered to Amanda's delicious breasts, the creamy curves swelling out of the low-cut neckline. 'If I were to ogle yours, *chérie*, I might forget myself!'

'I'd soon remind you!' she snapped, and he gave a derisive chuckle and extended his arm to her.

'What's that for?' She bent to examine the dark suiting.

'I'm taking you in to dinner!' he said. 'Didn't you learn *anything* at Herbert House?'

'Sure. That stable lads and estate workers make better gentlemen than the so-called nobs!'

With a long-suffering sigh, Piers pulled her hand through his arm and led her towards the dining-room.

As she glided gracefully beside him, she mulled over the best way of robbing him of his appetite. One thing for sure; if she couldn't figure out a way of doing so, her name wasn't Amanda Herbert!

The dining-room, though not large, was extremely pretty, with hand-painted eighteenth-century furniture that matched the elaborately carved ceiling, where gilded angels and cherubs romped. Two ormolu chandeliers glittered down on a table set with finely tooled silver cutlery and crystal goblets, a small white card bearing the name of a guest slotted into a tiny silver stand at every Limoges place-setting.

Amanda's initial disappointment at being seated diagonally opposite Piers, rather than next to him, gave way to pleasure as she realised that from this distance it would be impossible for him to hit her under the table!

The first course was cream of mussel soup, then when warm bread rolls were proffered she knew her chance had come. Everyone round her was carefully breaking theirs into pieces, but she ostentatiously picked up her dinner knife and slit hers in half, flashing Piers a bewitching smile as she did.

Tight-lipped, he deliberately broke off a small section of his roll, indicating, with a subtly down-pointed finger, that this was how it was done. Then, putting a piece in his mouth, he accompanied it with a spoonful of soup.

Feigning stupidity, Amanda cut her roll into smaller pieces still, then shovelled the lot into her soup bowl and stirred it round vigorously. She felt the elderly man on her left watching her with astonishment, while Piers looked ready to burst a blood vessel.

But she wasn't finished yet! The fillet of Dover sole defied her imagination, but the new potatoes that came with it provided her with a golden opportunity. Mashing every tender little one with her fork, she smothered the mound with butter and whisked it in vigorously.

'Is that how it's done in England?' the younger man on her right enquired, stopping in the midst of his interminable diatribe on fishing.

'There are lots of other ways,' she explained. 'But this one's my favourite.' Lifting her wine goblet in both her hands, she downed the contents at a gulp and smacked her lips.

She was now well into the swing of things and having a whale of a time. Relentlessly meat knife for fish was followed by fish knife for meat, while a dessertspoon was used to shovel up the tiny peas accompanying the lamb chops. She debated whether to eat the chops themselves with her fingers, even toyed with the idea of doing a Henry VIII and throwing the bones over her shoulder, but felt this might be more than Piers could take, so contented herself by holding the bone delicately with her napkin, and gnawing on it gustily.

To their credit, most of the guests ignored her behaviour, and Piers, finally accepting that nothing would stop her—short of hauling her from the room— maintained an admirable stoicism.

Deciding that enough was enough for the moment, Amanda tackled the praline ice cream and hothouse peaches with only a modicum of fuss, quietly pretending not to understand the talk around her, and stifling a laugh at a joke made in French.

Coffee was taken in the salon, with Piers glued to her side. 'You really surpassed yourself at dinner,' he savaged her. 'I've never seen such an appalling display of manners!'

'What did I do wrong?'

'It would be quicker to tell you what you did right! The sooner you have some lessons in manners the better. I'll come to your room tonight and——'

'Not likely! I know exactly what you're after!'

'Don't kid yourself,' he snarled. 'Just the thought of your behaviour turns me off!'

This was not what she wanted to hear, given that her aim was to make him crazy about her, and she vowed to behave herself tomorrow and set out to entice him.

'Don't let's quarrel, Piers,' she said softly, deciding now was as good a time as any to start. 'I'm doing me best, and it makes me miserable to think you don't like me.'

'I do like you,' he said hastily. 'It's simply that I find you—well—somewhat trying.'

Amanda wasn't surprised. Truth to tell, she had found *herself* trying! Indeed, she had had more than enough for one day. Her mother had been right when she had said acting on stage was easier than acting in a real-life situation, and all she yearned for at this moment was the peace and quiet of her room, where she could revert to her true self. But it was barely ten, and too early to leave a dinner-party that had been given in her honour.

Allowing herself a yawn, she pretended boredom at the ebb and flow of talk around her, and once again wished she'd had the foresight to say she'd been an au pair in France—or had had a French father. She hid a smile. How easily lies tripped from her tongue, and how gullibly Piers swallowed them!

Predictably, the insipid blonde he had chatted up before dinner wended her way over to them, and, throwing Amanda a perfunctory smile, took the armchair next to his. Piers immediately gave her his exclusive attention, and Amanda was furious not only at his neglect of her but at the girl's blatant flirtatiousness.

Irritably she took a gulp of coffee, almost spitting it out as it scalded her mouth. Leaning forward to set the cup on the low table in front of her, she saw a scarlet-tipped hand on Piers' knee. That did it! Pretending to lose her balance, Amanda sent her cup tilting on its side to splash brown liquid on the girl's dress. With a startled shriek the blonde leapt into the air, causing the stain to spread further.

'Oh dear!' Amanda squealed. 'I'm ever so sorry. You can throw your coffee over *me*, if it'll make you feel better!'

The girl was too busy swallowing her temper to reply, and a concerned Madame Dubray was instantly on the scene. 'Come to my room, Yvonne, I've some marvellous stuff that Henriette swears by.'

'Nothing will get out a coffee stain,' Yvonne wailed, giving Amanda a venemous look. 'My dress is ruined. Ruined!'

'If it is, we'll be happy to replace it,' Piers soothed. 'I'll even come with you to choose it!'

This drew a warm smile from Yvonne, who then allowed herself to be led away, and Amanda sat back again—aware of Piers' twitching mouth.

'Quite a temper, haven't you?' he murmured. 'That "accident" was deliberate.'

'I should have poured the coffee over *you*!'

'Pity you didn't. Knowing Yvonne, she'll drag me out tomorrow to buy her dress at double the price!'

Startled, Amanda looked at him, realising from his expression that he had found the incident amusing. How disarming he was when he gave humour free rein, she thought, and wished he did so more often with her.

Madame Dubray returned some minutes later minus Yvonne, saying the stain had been removed entirely, but that the dress was so wet that Lucien had driven her home.

The piercing glance Piers flung Amanda showed that his amusement hadn't faded, though as the evening wore on and the guests began to depart, he unexpectedly became taciturn again.

Instinct told her he was recollecting her behaviour at dinner, and, in no mood for a slanging match when the party was over, she determined to make for the safety of her room the instant she could.

The moment the door closed on the last guest, she headed smartly for the stairs, thwarted in her attempt to escape by Piers barring her way on the second step.

'Not so fast, my darling. Aren't you going to spend a few minutes alone with me?'

'I think that's my cue to wish you both good night,' Madame Dubray murmured tactfully behind them, and, smiling in anticipation of the tender love scene she was sure would ensue, went past them and up the stairs.

Silently Piers dragged Amanda into the small sitting-room and closed the door. 'I know you're not the brightest of girls,' he grated, 'but I suspect you're not quite the idiot you make out either.'

'What are you talking about?' she hedged.

'The act you put on tonight. I don't believe you didn't know what cutlery to use, and as for shovelling your roll into the soup and mashing up your potatoes . . .' Words failed him, and catching her shoulders he shook her as if she were a duster. 'Why do you pretend to be a moron when you aren't? What the hell's the matter with you?'

Amanda thought quickly, knowing that unless she gave him a satisfactory answer he would chew over the questions until he found the answers for himself.

'You treat me like a fool, so I behave like one,' she said.

Taken aback, his hands dropped to his sides. 'You're right. I guess I'm the fool. I should be helping you, not denigrating you. I guess I'm trying to mould you into something you can never be.'

'Wanting to turn a parrot into a sparrow,' she said huskily.

He couldn't restrain a chuckle. 'With your hair, a robin redbreast would be more like it!' Appraisingly he eyed her. 'If you only knew how much lovelier you look in subtle colours . . .'

'But I prefer bright ones,' Amanda said, managing to squeeze out a few tears.

At sight of them he flinched. 'Forgive me, Mandy. I've no right to criticise your taste. I've said some pretty harsh things to you, but they were for your own good.'

'For your good, you mean,' she sniffed miserably. 'That's all you care about. I don't mean a thing to you. I'm just a girl you hired to do a job, and when it's over and finished you won't give me another thought.'

'Won't I?' Frowning, he rubbed one long finger down the side of his chin. There was the slight rasp of stubble and she saw its faint blue shadow. It would be much darker in the morning, unless he shaved before going to bed.

'What are you thinking?' he asked, so abruptly that before she could stop herself she blurted it out.

Startled, he had to laugh. 'I only shave at night when I'm going to bed with someone. Satisfied?'

Colour swept Amanda's face. She hadn't blushed like this in years, and was furious with herself.

Seeing her red cheeks, he frowned again. 'I'm surprised you embarrass so easily.'

'I don't normally. But this is such a crazy situation and—and you're such a strange person . . .'

'So are you. One minute a fool, the next wise as the Oracles. She was the——'

'I know who she was!' Amanda snapped. 'I didn't go to a pricey private school like you, but I ain't illiterate!'

'There you go again!' he exclaimed. 'Getting uptight over nothing! I won't pretend we're alike, but that has nothing to do with our different backgrounds. I know plenty of girls who went to "pricey" schools with whom I've nothing in common.'

'Yet you'll end up marrying one of them,' Amanda flared. 'Someone like me would be out of the question!'

Unaccustomed embarrassment flitted across his face. 'I can't deny that, Mandy. Most of us prefer mixing with people who share our values and interests.'

'How do you know *I* don't? But you never give me a chance. It might have occurred to you to take me round the vineyards and explain what you do. I'm quick to learn, Piers. I can be anything you want.' Deliberately she raised her arms and pushed back her hair, the movement straining the bodice of her dress.

Piers' indrawn breath showed his awareness of the enticing swell, though his tone was clipped as he spoke. 'Right now I want you to carry on with our agreement and act as my fiancée.'

'And afterwards?' She ran the tip of her pink tongue along her soft lower lip.

'Afterwards, I . . .' His voice was thicker, huskier. 'Why think of afterwards, Mandy? What's wrong with now?'

His arms reached for her, and Amanda, mesmerised by the desire on his face, which mirrored her own, allowed herself to be pulled against him and drawn down to the settee, where he placed her back upon the cushions and then lay beside her.

'Maddening Mandy,' he whispered into her ear. 'Do you know what your body does to me?' His hand caressed her shoulder and moved lower to one full breast. 'It makes me forget about tomorrow,' he answered himself. 'Makes me believe there's only tonight, and that what happens now is all that matters.'

Lightly his fingers teased the erect point straining against the soft fabric of her dress, and with an incoherent murmur she turned her face to his and gave him her mouth. Instantly he set fire to it with his own, the piercing thrust of his tongue a white-hot flame that threatened to consume her. Deeper and deeper it went, and she trembled and clung to him, absorbed by his excitement and overwhelmed by her own, mindlessly answering kiss for kiss, touch for touch, until she felt the softness of fingertips along her inner thigh, moving up the satiny skin to the softness of hair.

Instantly she tensed, drawing her thighs together, and at the same time pushing away his hand.

'Am I going too fast for you?' he whispered thickly. 'I want you so badly I can't hold back much longer.'

The inference behind his words made her recoil, and she pushed him away so violently that he slipped off the settee to the floor.

'What the hell——' Startled, he stared up at her as she jumped angrily to her feet and straightened her dress. 'What's wrong, Mandy?'

'Your assumption that I was ready to go the whole way.' She was trembling with fury and racked by shame. 'All I did was kiss you back, yet you immediately think I'm . . . Oh, you make me sick!'

With easy grace Piers rose, buckling the crocodile belt of his pants as he did so.

'My mistake,' he said lightly. 'But all you had to do was say "no". I don't believe in rape.'

'I'm glad to hear it.' She was beginning to feel foolish for the scene she had made.

'In my defence,' he went on, 'you did rather give the impression you were willing. Still, no harm done.' Slipping on his jacket, he went to the door. 'Shall we go to bed? Our respective ones, I mean.'

Silently she preceded him out, and not until she was alone in the safety of her room did she acknowledge she was as much to blame as Piers for what had happened downstairs. She had flirted outrageously with him, and he had reacted to it as the playboy she knew him to be.

'So watch it,' she warned herself. 'You entered this game to teach Piers a lesson—not yourself!'

CHAPTER EIGHT

LUCIEN returned to Paris the day after the dinner-party, and for the remainder of the week Piers was fully occupied with the estate. Madame Dubray was involved with her local charities, and Amanda—mainly left to her own devices—rambled happily through the glorious gardens and spent absorbing hours in the library, careful not to let Piers see her in there.

'Poor Mandy,' he said on the Friday afternoon, bumping into her outside his study, where he had been closeted for hours with his estate manager. 'You must be bored out of your skull.'

Amanda swallowed a sharp retort. Let him be sorry for her!

'What do you do with yourself all day?' he went on.

'Count the blades of grass! I wish I could do something worthwhile.'

A dark eyebrow rose. 'Such as?'

'Dusting and cleaning.' She kept a straight face as she saw him wince.

'No fiancée of mine will do the domestic work here.'

'Then let me do something on the estate. I haven't even seen the vineyards yet.'

'There's nothing to see.'

'But you spend hours there!'

'Working, Mandy—not admiring the scenery.'

'Then let me work with you. I like helping things grow.'

'Me too,' he smiled, extending a hand to show her the scratches on his long supple fingers. 'But I don't think you'd be happy getting these.'

'I can wear gloves.'

'What a girl you are for nagging! But the answer's still "no".' He chucked her under the chin. 'Don't look so despondent. Lucien's coming down tomorrow, and we'll take you to lunch at La Fontaine; they do sensational quiches.'

So Lucien was coming here again. She found the news vaguely disquieting. 'Does he always come here so often?'

'No. I rather think you're the attraction.'

'Then you'd better act jealous.'

'Why?'

'Because you're supposed to be in love with me.'

'Ah yes, so I am. Okay, if he ogles you too passionately, I'll make suitable growling noises!'

Amanda sighed inwardly. Not even the thought of his friend fancying her could arouse Piers to anything more than flippancy. He started to walk away from her and she kept pace with him, surreptitiously taking in the black curls which, though ruthlessly brushed down, still managed to spring free on his forehead. He had caught the sun, too, and his skin glistened bronze, apart from a pale line at the nape of his neck.

He was in his 'working gear' of black slacks and sweater, though at night he always changed into smoking jackets—colourful ones of ruby velvet, or a blue several shades darker than his eyes—with white frilly shirts.

'That's rather an odd outfit,' his mother had commented only the night before, when he had appeared in a bottle-green jacket with gold embroidered shirt.

'It's Californian casual,' he had grinned, 'and what's more, over there it's considered conservative!'

His mother had shuddered, but Amanda had loved him in it. Well, perhaps not quite 'loved'; liked was more apt. Love and Piers didn't go together in her mind. Yet she would be less than honest if she didn't admit that when he turned his blue gaze on her, her pulse went haywire.

She scowled. The whole thing was becoming trickier than she had envisaged. The longer she played 'Mandy', the harder it was becoming to retain her own identity, and if she lost *that*, her emotions could fall foul of this highly attractive wolf. Which meant she had to bring him to heel damned quick and get out!

'Why so serious?' he questioned.

'I'm thinking of me future.'

'*My* future.'

'Me—my—what difference does it make? You talk so semantically.'

'Pedantically,' he chuckled.

'So I got it wrong,' she shrugged, 'but you know what I mean.'

'This time, yes. Most times not.'

She looked up and found him studying her, his expression showing appreciation of her subdued make-up and simple, cream cotton dress.

'You've fitted in very well here, Mandy. Surprisingly well, in fact. The staff like you—you've got Michel eating out of your hand, and I can't tell you how rare *that* is—and mother actually asked me if we've set the date for the wedding.'

Amanda could barely contain her triumph. 'You'd better watch out, or you might be stuck with me permanently!'

Expecting a playful retort, she was surprised when none came. Instead his brows drew together and his eyes darkened to indigo.

'There's no fear of that,' he said slowly. 'I happen to be in love with someone else.'

Startled, she stopped walking. 'Since when?'

'Since the past six months.'

Dismay coursed through her. 'But that day in the woods—when you hired me—you said you didn't intend marrying for years!'

'At the time I didn't know you well enough to confide my private feelings,' he replied. 'Apart from which, Hélène wants our engagement kept secret till she's qualified. She's studying architecture and has another year to go.'

Amanda regarded him with mounting fury. Had she known this she would never have agreed to his crazy offer. She started to tremble, feeling an intense desire to hurt him as much as he was hurting her. Yet why should she be hurt because a man who meant nothing to her was secretly engaged to someone else? She was simply angry with him for thwarting her plans.

'So now you know why I'm not afraid of being stuck with you,' Piers drawled into the silence.

She nodded, then said curiously, 'But why the secrecy? Making it official wouldn't stop your fiancée studying.'

'In her case it might. You see, her mother—who's something of a battle-axe, I'm afraid—would insist that she should quit college and marry me before I changed my mind!'

'Wise woman,' Amanda retorted.

'Not in this case. Hélène's a lovely girl, and I've every intention of waiting for her.'

'Does she know about me?'

'Yes.'

Hands on hips, Amanda gave him a scoffing look. 'I'd like to have seen her face when you told her.'

'She was highly amused.'

'She must have a great sense of humour, then.'

'She does.'

Amanda tried to picture the unknown Hélène. 'Where did you meet your ladylove?'

'Our families were neighbours until ten years ago, then her father died and she and her mother moved to Paris. I lost touch with her until last year when I met her at a dinner-party and knew instantly she'd be the ideal wife for me. Which is why I'm prepared to wait for her.'

And play around on the side, Amanda thought, remembering his conversation with Lucien on the terrace of Herbert House. The two-timing swine! Lining himself up a studious, well-bred French girl who'd clearly give him all the freedom he required, while at the same time providing him with a twenty-two-carat background!

The girl was indubitably an ice cube! What red-blooded female would be satisfied to let a man like Piers run loose when she could rope him in! The more Amanda thought about it, the more convinced she became that if she played her cards carefully *she* could rope him in instead. Then she'd tie him in knots and deliver him back to his ladylove!

'If I was engaged,' she stated, 'I wouldn't let the man out of me—out of my sight.'

'I bet you wouldn't,' Piers grinned. 'When you see something you want you go all out for it, don't you?'

'Absolutely. And talking of going,' she added slyly, 'I think it's time I did.'

'Why?' He was startled.

'Because I think you should come clean with your mother. I'm sure she'll keep your secret if you ask her.'

Piers raked his fingers through his hair, ruffling the front more than ever. 'There's more to it than that,' he confessed. 'You see, I don't want her to know I deceived her about *us*. She'd be terribly hurt.'

'Then how are we ever going to break it off?'

'Quite easily, if we do it from California. I'm going there next month, and ostensibly I'll be taking you with me. After a few weeks I'll write and say things didn't work out for us and we've called it a day. Then once I'm home I'll let a few months lapse before telling her about Hélène.'

'You've got it all worked out, haven't you?'

'Naturally.'

'And——'

'No more questions, Mandy. I have to go out.'

'May I come with you?'

'Afraid not. I've a lengthy session with my advertising agency, and I don't know when I'll be through.'

'Why do you need an advertising agency?'

'To promote our wine. These days it isn't enough to produce a superlative growth, we also have to make the public aware of it.'

'The power of the media,' she muttered, and his startled glance told her she'd forgotten herself again. 'I ain't just a pretty face,' she added.

'I know. You've many hidden depths, Mandy.'

'Which is why I plan to better myself. Staying here has given me a taste for this kind of life.' She parted her lips, the tip of her tongue snaking out to moisten them. A muscle flickered in his jaw and she lowered her lids to hide her amusement. 'What time will you be back for dinner?' she asked softly.

'I won't. But I haven't forgotten my promise to take you out to lunch tomorrow.'

It was no compensation for not seeing him this evening, and she gave a pouting sigh as she watched him go.

Noon next day found her waiting for him by his car. Her lavender cotton dress enhanced the delicacy of her features, making one less aware of her bright orange hair, which she had ruthlessly brushed free of frizz and pulled back in a pony tail.

Expecting a compliment from Piers, she was disappointed when, with barely a glance at her, he strode down the steps and took his place behind the wheel.

'Where are we meeting Lucien?' she asked, getting in beside him.

'At the restaurant. I called him when I got back last night.'

His tone was curt, telling her he was in no mood for small talk, and she lapsed into silence, though she would have given a great deal to know what was bugging him.

But his spirits lifted as they came to the village of La Fontaine and he stopped outside the restaurant of the same name—an inordinately grand one, Amanda thought, for such a tiny hamlet. But then, this was France, where magnificent restaurants were often found in the most out-of-the-way places.

She wasn't surprised to see crowds milling around the flower-filled garden and packing the tables on the terrace, though Piers, predictably, had only to give his name for them to be ushered to a table in a plum position, its white linen cloth dappled with the faint green shadows of the thick leaves of an old vine which trailed in among the overhead beams. It was an enchanting setting. Floral garden, bustling waiters laden with trays, smiling, contented diners. Amanda wouldn't have been surprised to see Manet and his easel behind the flowering laurel, eagerly recording the scene for posterity.

'Penny for your thoughts,' Piers asked.

She'd love to see his face if she told him! 'I was wondering where Lucien is,' she lied. 'I'm starving.'

'Have a roll.'

'I'd prefer a glass of wine.'

'I thought you couldn't stand the stuff.'

'It's a woman's prerogative to change her mind.' She watched as he ordered a bottle of Chablis, noting how the waitress flirted with him, and how smoothly charming he was to her in return.

'Lucien's late,' he grunted as they started on their second glass.

'Hope you ain't bored with me,' Amanda said.

'On the contrary,' came the grudging admission. 'You've a nice sense of humour and a refreshing way of looking at things.'

'Different from you, you mean?'

'Different from most girls, and utterly unpredictable.'

'I thought that scared you to death!'

'It did once,' he smiled. 'But it has its compensations.'

'Which are?'

'That you don't bore me!'

'That's what Lucien said.'

Piers' comment was forestalled by the subject of their discussion coming towards them with a stunning brunette in tow.

'Mariette—what a surprise!' Piers jumped up. 'Lucien didn't say he was bringing you!'

'A spur of the moment decision,' his friend replied. 'We bumped into each other at the Crillon, and when Mariette mentioned she was on her way to St Tropez, I suggested she should break her journey here.'

'I won't inflict myself on you, Piers darling,' the girl drawled. 'I'll book into a hotel. It's simply that I couldn't resist the chance of seeing you again and meeting your fiancée.'

'I'm glad you didn't. And I won't hear of your going to a hotel. We've room enough at the château.' His eyes appraised her. 'You look marvellous.'

The whole restaurant seemed to agree, Amanda thought sourly, for all eyes were riveted on the dark-haired, curvaceous woman, whose eyes were as vivid a blue as Piers'. In a white dress that clung lovingly to every swell and indentation, she was the epitome of every man's dream—and knew it!

'It's been ages since I've seen you,' she was drawling huskily to him, and she placed her ruby red mouth on his in a brief, open-mouthed kiss.

Amanda wanted to hit her. How dare she kiss him like that in front of her? In an uprush of rage, she gave Piers a sharp kick on the shin.

'What's that for?' he demanded, swinging round on her.

'For not introducing me, sweetie.'

'You must blame me for that,' Mariette intervened in faultless English. 'I took Piers by surprise.' She held out a hand. 'I'm Mariette Boudin, and you must be Mandy.'

'Too right,' Amanda said. 'Did you really break your journey especially to meet me?'

'Of course. I couldn't wait to see the girl who'd finally captured one of France's most eligible bachelors. You're very lucky, you know.'

'My friends would say that to *him*!' Amanda cooed.

'And they'd be right,' Piers said, then spoiled it by giving his undivided attention to the French girl.

Feigning unconcern, Amanda concentrated on Lucien, though remaining acutely aware of the couple beside her. In the eyes of one the fires still burned—for Mariette's body trembled with desire—though in the eyes of the other she could discern nothing.

But that didn't make Piers immune, for he was a sensual man and needed his sexual appetite appeasing—and Mariette looked as if she were no mean appeaser! With an effort Amanda kept rein on her temper, though not so successfully on her imagination, which was bombarded with images she had no wish to explore.

'I hope you don't think I've come to take Piers away from you?' Mariette uncannily sensed Amanda's thoughts.

'Mandy's not the jealous sort,' Piers interjected slyly, and Amanda knew he was remembering the spilled coffee at the dinner party. 'In fact, she enjoys meeting my friends.'

'In that case, why not come to St Tropez for a few days?' Mariette suggested.

'That's not a bad idea. How about it, Mandy my sweet?'

Although the south of France with Piers sounded enticing, the prospect was ruined by the thought of sharing him with a girl she was beginning thoroughly to dislike. I must be going nuts! she admonished herself. Why should I *feel* jealous, when I'm only supposed to be acting it? Yet feeling it she definitely was.

'Well, Mandy?' Piers repeated. 'Fancy the idea?'

'Sounds smashing. But didn't we come here to be with your mother?'

Appreciating the inference, Piers turned to Mariette. 'Mandy's right. It's no go, I'm afraid.'

'Poor darling,' the French girl commiserated. 'And you've always been bored with the rustic life.'

'Not true,' he corrected. 'Cities are fine when you're single, but you can't beat the country for raising a family.'

'A family?' Carefully plucked eyebrows rose. 'I can't see you enjoying squalling children and wet nappies.'

'Then you're very short-sighted,' Amanda put in.

'Long-sighted, I think,' Mariette said silkily, and Piers laughed at Amanda.

'Can *you* see me changing nappies and giving bottles?'

'For your own children, yes. You love watching things grow, and you'll find babies more rewarding than vines!'

'You'll make a beautiful mother,' Lucien murmured.

'Right now she happens to be my fiancée,' Piers reminded him edgily, and his friend, remembering Mariette's presence, kept his mouth shut.

As she watched Lucien, it occurred to Amanda that he had brought Mariette here to show 'Mandy' that Piers was a womaniser and not to be trusted. On the other hand, wouldn't it have been simpler just to tell her about Hélène? Or didn't Hélène exist? Was she simply a figment of Piers' imagination, a barrier he had dreamed up to hide behind? The first chance she had, she would ask Lucien.

Her opportunity came when they gave their order for lunch, for as he had done in the restaurant in Paris he leaned close to translate the menu for her.

'Do you know Hélène le Blanc?' she asked very quietly.

'Hélène? Why, yes. But I haven't seen her in years. Why the interest?'

'Piers mentioned her yesterday.'

'He probably associates her with Amanda. Hélène also had a crush on him when she was a kid. Except that she was very pretty.'

'How old is she now?'

'Early twenties, I think.'

'I've a feeling Piers fancies her,' Amanda murmured.

'I doubt it. He saw her not long ago and said she was like a rose without scent.'

'And Piers clearly goes for scent!'

'The more exotic the better. Now the scent of you . . .' Lucien breathed, and leaned even closer.

' "Joy",' she said prosaically. 'Any girl can smell the same if she has the money.'

To Amanda's relief, the maître's gentle cough brought Lucien's attention back to the menu, leaving her free to ponder on what she had learned—that Hélène did indeed exist, but that Piers had clearly invented his engagement to her in order to protect himself from 'Mandy', as he was using Mandy to protect himself from Lady Amanda! What a web of deceit he was weaving around himself, and what fun it would be to strangle him in it!

The thought brought back her appetite, and she tucked into the assortment of mouth-watering little quiches set before her, her brain buzzing with more ways of bringing this arrogant man to his knees—but in front of her, with a proposal on his lips!

CHAPTER NINE

IT was early afternoon when they made their way back through the leafy countryside to the château—Mariette in Lucien's car and Amanda in Piers'—and as they cruised down the winding drive, softly shaded by beech, Amanda experienced a strange sense of homecoming as disconcerting as it was unexpected.

They found Madame Dubray relaxing under a vast sunshade on the upper lawn, and she smiled as they approached, greeting Lucien with warm affection and Mariette with cool charm.

What must she think of the odd assortment of women her son brings home? Amanda mused. First, a garishly adorned country bumpkin, then a pseudo-sophisticated vixen, and Lord knew who else! Little wonder that Amanda Herbert, buck teeth and all, had appealed to her sense of safety!

'Any suggestions for this afternoon?' Piers asked from the depths of his garden chair.

'I fancy a game of tennis,' Mariette said promptly.

Piers quirked an eyebrow at Mandy. 'Do you play?'

'Well, I ain't no Martina what's-her-name,' she came back pertly, 'but I can hit a ball over the net.'

'I think we should wait till it's cooler,' Lucien ventured, and Amanda knew he was trying to protect her. He really was a poppet—worth two of his arrogant friend!

'Piers and I can play singles,' Mariette said.

'Stuff that!' Amanda came back. 'I'm ready when you are.'

'You'd best partner me, then,' Piers said. 'I'll do the running for us both.'

Mariette looked at him sullenly, and Amanda's

90

dislike of her intensified. What a foul creature! She
had to be marvellous in bed if Piers could bother with
her out of it! Pushing the thought aside, she followed
the men to the games room to select a racquet and
plimsolls.

'Lucien tells me you and Piers have only just got
engaged,' Mariette said, beside her. 'Where did you
meet?'

Afraid to put her foot in it, for she didn't know
exactly what Lucien had said, Amanda feigned
deafness, and rushed ahead of the girl to the tennis
court. She waited while a coin was flipped for service,
net height checked and a box of balls opened and
tested, debating all the while what game to play. Her
normal one would be too dangerous, for no-one would
believe it of 'Mandy'. So what then? Be the complete
novice and miss every ball? That didn't appeal either.
Maybe she'd opt for something between the two.

They knocked up—Amanda deliberately missing
most of the shots, and hiding a smile as Piers raised his
eyes heavenwards.

Winning the toss for service, he sent the ball
whizzing across the net. They won that game hands
down, Piers obviously deciding that, since he was
virtually going it alone, he'd give the game everything
he had.

The next one went to Lucien and Mariette, with
Amanda still contributing virtually nothing. Then it
was her turn to serve. Resisting the urge to slam the
ball across the net, she contented herself with a
ladylike display of patball, accompanied by a simpering
smile at Lucien each time he praised her for getting
one in. Maintaining this level of play for the following
three games, she was grateful to Piers for his
incredible speed and stretch, which saved her the
over-riding temptation of whacking a return straight at
Mariette.

The French girl and Lucien were excellent

opponents, but Amanda knew that with her normal
game she could have wiped the floor with them. What
she'd give to see their faces if she did!

'You're doing fine,' Lucien encouraged her as they
changed sides.

'You mean Piers is,' Mariette interposed. 'He might
as well be playing on his own!'

'Might as well be playing on his own?' Amanda
didn't have auburn hair for nothing. She'd wipe the
smirk off Mariette's face if it was the last thing she
did! Fortunately it was her turn to serve, and she
threw the ball in the air with an effortless swing and
spun it across the net at the other girl. With a shocked
look on her face, Mariette watched it swerve past her.

'That had a spin on it!' she cried.

'Nonsense!' Piers said.

Amanda stifled a smile, careful to send an ordinary
serve across to Lucien, which she managed to drop
just inside the service line. It came back fast and low
and, shrieking at Piers to get out of the way, she
slammed it across at Mariette, missing her by a hair's-
breadth.

All three stared at Amanda.

'Incredible shot,' Lucien gasped.

'A fluke,' she shrugged, and from then on subtly
spun her every serve to the other girl.

Mariette missed all but one of them, growing so
flustered and angry that Piers, with ill-concealed
amusement, called out, 'Seems Mandy's too good for
you!'

Amanda forced an ingenuous expression, then
played two more outstanding ground strokes that
helped to win her and Piers set and match.

Piers' mouth quirked with humour as he con-
gratulated her, though his comment was laconic. 'You
must have had some pretty good training. A bit more
practice and you'd make Wimbledon!'

Tossing her head, she preceded him off the court.

'I've better things to do with my time than hit a ball backwards and forwards across a net.'

'Sweeping and dusting, I presume?'

'What's wrong with that?'

'Nothing. I'm not deriding domestic work, Mandy, but if you've other talents you should use them.'

'You think I've other talents, then?'

'Yes. And your biggest is rubbing me up the wrong way!'

'And my littlest?'

She was deliberately riling him, curious to see if he would rise to the bait. But he didn't, and sauntered across to Mariette, who was still nursing a bruised ego.

'Let's cool off with a swim,' he suggested.

Instantly her face lit up, and Amanda, knowing she couldn't bear watching them wallow in the pool, announced that she was going to her room to shower.

'Don't tell me you can't swim?' Piers remarked pointedly.

'I'm an excellent swimmer,' she retorted with such bravura that she knew he didn't believe her, and with a toss of her head she stalked away.

Cool after her shower, and wearing one of her pretty Parisian sundresses, Amanda stood gazing out the window at the sweep of lawns and the deep green of shrubbery marking its boundary. Beyond it she glimpsed the deeper green of one of the vineyards, the vines set in regimented rows on their carpet of brown soil. How lovingly nurtured and cared for they were. Pity Piers didn't bestow the same concern on his women!

But why should he when they were happy to accept him as he was? Turning back into the room, she wondered if he would ever marry and, when he did, if he would continue to lead his own life on the side. Well, that wasn't her problem. All that concerned her was what he did with it in the next few days.

The thought of leaving the château filled her with

an unexpected sense of sadness that grew more
overwhelming with each step she took along the
corridor. Despite its size, it was very much a home,
nearly all its lovely rooms in constant use—apart from
the nursery suite in the west wing turret. It was here
that Amanda had spent a great deal of time this past
week, drawn to it like a magnet, as if, surrounded by
Piers' childish things, she would more clearly envisage
him as a child too.

Lost in thought, she went outside and strolled along
a quiet pathway bordered by dense foliage, until she
unexpectedly found herself on a narrow dirt road
bordering the vineyard she had seen from her window.
Everywhere around her bunches of hard, small green
grapes gave promise of plump juicy ones to come, and
her mouth watered at the prospect. Wandering
between the vines, she felt an overwhelming yearning
to have Piers close. Not only here and now, but always
and for ever.

Always and for ever? Oh Lord! How could she have
been so blind? Every emotion Piers had aroused in
her—rage, amusement, contempt, liking—suddenly
jelled into one frightening realisation.

She loved him.

Illogically, foolishly, she had fallen for this most
selfish of men. She, who had always regarded herself
as a liberated woman of the eighties, was lovesick for a
chauvinist who still saw women as playthings.

Shocked by the revelation, she was powerless to
move. Her mother had been right to warn her of the
dangerous game she was playing. Jokes all too often
rebounded on the joker—as this one could well do on
her! After all, 'Mandy', despite her cockney accent and
orange hair, was still Amanda, and as such should
have roused Piers to more than the almost contemp-
tuous passion he had shown for her on the night of the
dinner-party. Even Lucien held her in more regard.
The trouble was, it wasn't Lucien she loved.

She walked on, trying to rationalise her feelings. What did Piers have to offer that other men didn't? The château and its vineyards? A lifestyle to match hers? She frowned, realising that her love for him had nothing to do with possessions, and that it stemmed from a need that only he could fulfil.

A soft rustle intruded into her thoughts and she stopped—aghast as she saw she had nearly stepped on a small grey bird. One wing flurried pitifully, the other hung limp at its side.

'Poor little thing.' She bent to touch it.

It shivered as she did, and, carefully cupping her palm round it, she lifted it up and tenderly stroked its breast, cooing to it consolingly. So absorbed was she, that not until a dark shadow fell across her did she glance up and see Piers.

'What are you holding?' he asked.

'A bird. It's hurt its wing.'

'Let me see.'

'Be gentle with it.'

'I'm always gentle with birds.' Carefully he took it from her. 'Particularly the female of the species!'

'How do you know it's female?' she sniffed, ignoring the remainder of his comment.

'From its markings.' Lightly he touched the wing. 'It'll be fine. I'll take it to Michel. He's got healing hands.'

Amanda stroked the tiny head.

'Lucky bird,' Piers murmured, and her heart leapt wildly as she saw the warm glow in his eyes. 'I mean, lucky that you happened to be passing,' he added. 'What are you doing here anyway? The grapes aren't ready to eat yet.'

'I know. I just came to look. Besides, I like the silence here. It has a strange timelessness.'

'That's what my mother says. I suppose she told you?'

'Don't you think I'm capable of my own feelings?'

Amanda demanded. 'Or do you enjoy making out I'm an idiot?'

'Of course I don't. Though you often pretend you're one! I can't fathom you, Mandy.'

Delighted that he was seeing beneath the surface she presented to him, she felt happiness burgeoning inside her. Maybe all was not lost. With a little push he might yet fall for Mandy, and the moment he did, she'd confess all.

'Let's take the bird to Michel,' he said, and turned so swiftly that she had the impression he was running away from something. His feelings, perhaps?

'Piers, wait! I want to talk to you.' She was suddenly determined to end the charade here and now.

'What is it?' he muttered, still walking.

Before she had a chance to speak, Mariette emerged from the shrubbery, a silk kimono swirling sensuously round her and barely concealing a minuscule bikini.

'What are you holding, Piers?' she asked.

'Come and see for yourself,' he drawled, moving towards her, and as the two dark heads bent over his palm Amanda beat a hasty retreat to the château, thankful she had not had a chance to confess.

It looked as if Piers still had his lesson to learn, and not until he succumbed fully to 'Mandy', and admitted he loved her, would she divulge her identity. But oh, how she hoped it would be soon.

CHAPTER TEN

AMANDA flung open her wardrobe and stared at the small but elegant range of clothes Piers had bought her. But it didn't matter what she wore. Mariette would ensure he had eyes for no one but herself! Yet why should she kowtow to this predatory female? She was playing a part, and she would play it to the full!

With a smile she lifted out a black crêpe evening dress. It was totally wrong for a cosy dinner at home, but needs must when the devil drove—and Mariette was unquestionably the devil!

Thirty minutes later, her reflection told her she had never looked more stunning—with the deeply plunging neckline revealing the curve of her breasts, and the draped skirt clinging to her rounded stomach and shapely hips, before falling in graceful folds to high-heeled silver sandals.

Yet she was still not satisfied. Turning this way and that, she realised what was missing: the neckline cried out for some jewellery.

But what? With a mischievous grin she rummaged in her drawer until she found the bright piece of Woolworth glass she had kept as a talisman from her childhood. Slipping it round her throat, she carefully hid the cheap-looking clasp beneath her fall of hair. The glass bauble took on a magical quality against her skin—a twenty-carat diamond to say the least, and enough to knock out Mariette's envious eyes! Earrings were still called for, though, and within seconds long drop ones with the same fake sparkle—loaned her by the real Mandy—dangled from her ears. Great! She looked a million dollars—literally!

The antique clock on the marble mantelpiece told

her it was time to go down, but she held back, intent on making a late and spectacular entrance, which she admirably achieved some quarter of an hour later when, gliding sinuously into the sitting-room, two casually-garbed men and a trouser-suited Mariette greeted her with stunned silence.

'Are we supposed to be going to some party?' Piers enquired with veiled sarcasm.

' 'Course not,' Amanda trilled. 'I just wanted to look me best.'

His eyes ranged over her, homing in on the glittering pendant round her throat and the sparkling glass swinging from her lobes.

'Smashing, ain't they?' she beamed at the room at large. 'Piers' present to me.'

Mariette looked ready to burst with envy, while Lucien, taken in by what he took to be a king's ransom, remained speechless. Only Piers looked worried that she was up to something he wasn't going to like.

She sauntered across to him and slipped an arm through his. 'Go on, ducky, tell your friends why I'm wearing them.'

'To give Mariette a heart attack,' he said, so quietly that only she could hear, and more loudly added, '*You* tell them, sweetheart. I can see you're dying to.'

She spun round to her audience. 'It's our anniversary. Two weeks ago today we became engaged.'

'What a generous man you're marrying,' Mariette said in dulcet tones. 'But you should be careful about wearing those diamonds in public—you'd be a prime target for terrorists.'

Giving her a withering look, Amanda fluttered her lashes at Piers. He tensed, the darkening of his tan showing his awareness of her body pressing against his jacket, the warm musky smell of her, the provocation of her full mouth which she deliberately let tremble.

Sapphire eyes remained riveted to grey ones, and his breathing became audibly faster.

'You're a bitch,' he said softly, and looping her hair up one side of her head, spoke into her ear. 'What's this new game you're playing, Mandy?'

'I'm just giving Mariette a stay-off sign.'

'You couldn't have done it better! For two pins, I'd put you over my knee and spank you.'

'Oh goody! Is that your fetish?'

'It could very well become that with you.'

Madame Dubray's entry saved Amanda from replying. For an instant the woman was taken aback at the sight of Amanda in all her sparkling glory, then with commendable aplomb she recovered herself.

'My dear, how—how lovely you look. You put us all to shame.'

'I wasn't trying to,' Amanda smiled, and once again found that playing a joke on Piers—if it meant fooling his mother—was no fun.

'I suppose you've seen your son's engagement present to Mandy?' Mariette asked her hostess.

The older woman's eyes went instantly to the pendant, then lifted to Amanda's, the twinkle in them obvious.

'Almost as lovely as the wearer,' she murmured, then glanced quickly at her son. 'I think it's time we went into dinner, don't you?'

Only too happy at the change of subject, Piers led them out to the terrace, where a table had been set with fresh salmon, and an assortment of salads.

What could be nicer, Amanda thought, than a superb meal in superb surroundings, with two handsome men—one of whom she adored—and a charming hostess? Only Mariette's presence spoiled it. Momentarily she thought of what it would be like married to Piers and living here. Yet, though the château was beautiful, she knew that being with him in a shack would make her equally happy.

'Penny for your thoughts,' Lucien broke into her reverie.

With a start she returned to the present, and, aware of Mariette listening, said, 'I was wondering how I'll keep myself occupied when I'm here permanently.'

'Hardly permanently,' Piers put in. 'We'll be spending half our time in the Napa Valley.'

'So we will. Gosh, imagine me going to America!'

'When are you actually getting married?' Mariette asked. 'Or is yours one of those on-going engagements?'

'I'm not that sort of girl!' Amanda snorted, and leaned towards Piers. 'When *are* we getting married, darling? I'll need to choose a dress and decide on bridesmaids.'

'Forget the bridesmaids. I've no intention of having a big wedding.'

'Really, Piers!' his mother expostulated. 'Don't Mandy's wishes count too?'

'I'm sure she'll do whatever makes me happy, Maman.'

'Not when it comes to my wedding, I won't,' Amanda stated. 'I want a slap-up do with a three-tiered cake.'

'We'll discuss it later,' Piers grated.

From the corner of her eye Amanda saw Mariette smirk, and knew the girl was conscious of the tension existing between herself and Piers. Deciding to remedy the situation, Amanda edged her chair closer to his and caressed his hand. His skin was cool to her touch, and she wondered what it would be like to lie close to him and caress his body.

The thought made her cheeks burn and she gave him a sidelong glance to see if he was aware of her tension. But he was preoccupied in dealing with his own, for a nerve was twitching visibly at his temple, and his jaw was clenched tight. A pang of love—pure and intense—shot through her, and she was hard put not to fling her arms round him.

As darkness fell and the lights on the terrace came on, the whine of insects drove them inside, where coffee and liqueurs were served. Not long after, Madame Dubray excused herself, saying she wanted an early night, at which point Mariette suggested they should put on some music and dance.

Obligingly Piers complied, and drew Mariette into his arms, holding her so close that a sheet of paper could barely have slipped between them!

Amanda was furious that he hadn't asked *her* first, and resisted the urge to pull them apart, knowing she would be playing into the girl's hands if she did—and Piers' too—for he was clearly doing it to show he was still his own man.

'Come on,' Lucien said beside her, pulling her to her feet, 'let's show those two what real dancing is.'

'To this music?'

'We'll change it.'

Moving across to the compact disc player, he flipped swiftly through the pile of discs, grinning as he selected one and slipped it in. The pulsating beat of a Fifties boogie-woogie boomed through the room, tinkling the glass chandeliers, and he held out his arms to Amanda.

Instantly she went into them. She had always loved dancing, and as a child had trained for the ballet until her height had made it impossible. But it hadn't stopped her from pursuing other forms of dance, and tonight she would have outshone Ginger Rogers herself, her suppleness and inventive movements lifting Lucien to heights he had never dreamed of. Indeed, as the beat reached a crescendo, he whirled her above his head, slid her down his back, and spun her to a stop!

Gasping for breath, she leaned against him, her heart racing as fast as his.

'Fantastic!' Mariette applauded. 'Ever danced in the chorus, Mandy?'

'Sure. I was a dance hostess too, till Piers bought all me tickets!'

Mariette glanced swiftly at the man still holding her. She knew she was being kidded, yet was also aware that Mandy was not the type she would have associated with him. 'Where *did* you two meet? I still don't know.'

'At Herbert House,' he replied suavely. 'We were both there one weekend.'

'You mean the house you're going to inherit?'

He nodded curtly, and crossed the room to put on some softer music.

Amanda waited for him to ask her to dance, but again he drew Mariette into his arms, and once more Amanda controlled her anger.

'Beats me what Piers is up to,' Lucien muttered in her ear. 'Anyone would think he still fancies Mariette.'

'Maybe he does.'

'Never. It was over years ago. And it only lasted a few months, anyway. But she's never given up hope.'

'Is that why you brought her here?'

Lucien had the grace to redden. 'I simply thought you should see you've no chance of hooking Piers permanently.'

'What makes you think I want to?' she snorted, anxious not to give away her feelings.

'Does that mean *I* have a chance with you when you leave here?'

'Depends what you have to offer,' she said, speaking loudly enough for Piers to hear as he danced past them. The tight line of his mouth showed he had, and, delighted, she pressed herself closer to Lucien. But they had only taken a few steps when—'*My* dance, I think,' Piers said from behind her—and in one swift movement whirled Mariette into Lucien's arms and herself into his.

At the touch of his hands, Amanda became alight, her pulse soaring, her feet barely seeming to touch the ground, yielding breasts against unyielding chest, soft, curving hips against hard thighs. No need for music for their bodies to move in unison; passion performed its own throbbing rhythm. Piers' chin pressed down on her head, then lower until his cheek touched hers. She could not control her trembling, or her hands from pulling him closer still. God! how she wanted him; ached for his mouth on hers, to have his hands roam her body.

'You're not only a bitch,' he whispered, 'you're a witch, and you've got me under your spell.'

'You could have fooled *me*.'

'It was meant to fool Mariette,' he said.

'How mean of you!'

'No meaner than you with Lucien. He's not your type, Mandy.'

So Piers was jealous! Happiness bubbled inside her like milk on a flame. But she mustn't let it boil over yet, and she eased slightly away from him.

'Scared?' he asked softly.

'Tired,' she lied. 'Time for bed.'

'*My* sentiments entirely.'

'*Alone,*' she emphasised.

'That's where we differ!' He stepped back from her. 'Mandy and I are turning in,' he announced.

'Me too,' Lucien agreed.

'What's wrong with all of you?' Mariette snapped. 'The evening's just begun!'

'You can watch some video if you like,' Piers suggested.

'No, thanks.' Scowling, she followed them upstairs.

Amanda was curious to see if Piers would escort Mariette to her room, and was wondering how she'd react if he did, when she found him turning with her into the west wing and calling 'good night' over his shoulder to the others. Hiding her elation she went on

walking unconcernedly till she reached her bedroom
door, and, hand on the knob, waited for him to move
on. But he remained beside her, overpoweringly close.

'Good night, Piers,' she said, keeping her eyes down
as she inched open the door.

'Not so fast.' Pushing it wider, he propelled her in,
then shut it behind them. 'We have to talk.'

'What about?'

'You and me. You don't own me, Mandy, and I
don't want you to forget it.'

Mortified that she had misunderstood his intention,
her temper rose. 'Own you? I wouldn't have you as a
gift in a packet of cornflakes!'

'You didn't give that impression downstairs.'

'Because I wanted to annoy Mariette. And if you ask
me, I was doing you a favour—unless you're planning
to start up with her again?'

'I don't need any favours from you, thanks. I'm
quite capable of warding off predatory females—and
that includes *you*!'

'Why, you—you conceited swine!'

'Because I think you fancy me?'

'I'm *supposed* to fancy you, you idiot! It's what
you're paying me for.' Too late she saw the gleam in
his eye, and as she backed away he caught her round
the waist. 'Let me go.'

'Not yet. You're my loving fiancée, remember? And
a little kiss in return for diamonds worth a king's
ransom isn't much to ask, is it?' Grasping her hair, he
pulled her head back and brought his face down to
hers.

Amanda remained motionless, though every inch of
her cried out for him. 'Men who try to seduce
unwilling girls went out with Queen Victoria,' she said
calmly.

'*Are* you unwilling? I didn't think so the night of
the party, and now I'm convinced of it. Anyway, all
I'm asking for is a kiss.'

'Not likely!'

'Very likely!' he grunted, and brought his mouth hard down on hers.

His pent-up emotion—brought on by her relentless teasing of him this past week—erupted into a fiery, uncontrollable passion, his teeth grinding against hers, the pressure of his mouth forcing her lips apart. Instantly his tongue penetrated the moist depth, and she gasped and clutched at him wildly. Of its own volition, her tongue entwined with his, and as the rhythmic movements gathered momentum, the ruthless onslaught of his mouth grew tender and more gently invasive, drawing the sweet moisture from hers, and filling her with his own.

Deftly his hands roamed her body, her silky dress no barrier to his questing fingers. There was the sound of a zip being drawn, and her dress dropped, exposing her high, full breasts. Easing his mouth from hers, he lowered his head and began to suck the stiff, red nipples rising from the creamy skin.

'God! you're beautiful,' he groaned, and lowered her zip further, till the dress slithered in folds to her feet. Lifting her out of them, he carried her to the bed, his eyes ranging over her body as he placed her gently upon it. Throwing off his shirt and stepping out of his slacks, he came down beside her.

'Such pretty panties,' he murmured, his finger snaking between her skin and the shirred elastic, 'but it won't do as a chastity belt!'

'I've an iron will, though,' she came back at him, and his eyes lit with amusement.

'Never lost for an answer, are you, Mandy?'

His mouth gentled hers, though his hands were firm as they began fondling every curve and indentation, ceasing only as they reached the innermost crevice and she tensed.

'No?' he whispered.

'No.'

'But I want you.'

'I guessed that!' Fleetingly her fingers touched the hardness against her thigh.

'Why not?' he persisted. 'We're adults, aren't we, and I assume you're on the pill?'

She wasn't, but had no intention of telling him. If he knew she had only been to bed with one man, and then only because she'd believed they would marry, he would roar with laughter.

'Don't refuse me,' he pleaded, his mouth finding hers again, his hands sliding over the silken tautness of her stomach before returning to the downy mound nestling below.

He played with the hairs and she shivered ecstatically, yearning to part her legs for him, but knowing that, if she allowed him to enter her, her true feelings would be revealed to him. Yet she did not have the strength of mind to reject him utterly, and she needed to savour this moment lest it never came again. The Amanda who'd been so confident of bringing Piers to heel no longer existed, and her biggest fear was that once they left the château *she* would cease to exist for him too.

'Piers,' she whispered huskily, her trembling hands moving across his broad shoulders, the supple spine, the hard curve of his buttocks, then round his hips to stroke his stomach, feeling a shudder go through him as she did.

Her touch set him alight, and his manhood swelled and pressed hard into her thigh, its throbbing heat as fierce as the heat coursing through her. God! how she needed him inside her! To fill her with his seed, to flood every part of her being with his very essence.

I love you, she cried silently, glad she had the control not to cry it aloud, and sorry she hadn't the control to push him away.

As though aware of her dilemma he held her closer, then raised himself and eased her under him, his sinewy legs straddling her, his arms supporting his weight lest he crush her.

'Don't stop me,' he said raggedly, his eyes burning into hers. 'I want you so much I can't think straight. You've been a thorn in my flesh since I met you, Mandy, and you've dug yourself so deep I can't get you out.'

They were words she had longed to hear him say, though the vital one was still missing—love!

He spoke only of 'need' and 'desire', the urge to appease the passion raging through him. But did he think he could do it by bedding her? And if she gave in to him, wouldn't it be 'bye bye, Mandy, and thanks for the memory'?

The knowledge that this could happen gave her the willpower to resist him, and with a swift wriggle she slid out from under him.

Taken by surprise he remained where he was, an eyebrow quirked in a question-mark which she answered by pulling the sheet up to cover her.

'Please go, Piers.'

'You don't mean that.'

'I do.'

Slowly he rose, his skin gleaming in the shaded light. He reached for his shirt and briefs, his muscles rippling like silken cords, and her fascinated eyes moved lower, her fingers yearning to splay themselves across his flat stomach, to encompass the thick bulge he so unconcernedly left uncovered.

Aware that she was watching him, he spoke. 'I'm sorry you said no. We'd make beautiful music together.'

'I don't care for pop songs that are here today and gone tomorrow.'

'It's the music of the Eighties.'

'Then I'm not an Eighties girl.'

He zipped up his slacks and came towards her, his eyes riveted to the outline of her breasts, making her aware that even through the cotton covering her erect nipples were her give-away.

'You can't deny you want me,' he said.

'But not as a pop song. I'm looking for something more lasting.'

'Really? Little girls who play for high stakes could end up impaled on them!'

'I'll take that chance.' She pulled the sheet higher. 'Don't you ever get bored with pop music, Piers?'

'Not so far. It's enjoyable while it lasts, but is easily forgotten—and that suits me fine.'

His answer was the biggest turn-off he could have given her, and silently she thanked him for it. As her desire for him ebbed, her wits grew sharper.

'Where does Hélène figure in all this,' she asked, delighted to see him tense. Let him get out of *that* one!

'She doesn't,' he said slowly. 'She's a symphony, and once I start listening to that kind of music there'll be no other for me.'

'I can be a symphony too, for the right man.'

'I'm sure you can.'

Piers' expression was unreadable as their eyes met. Then she saw the blue slowly lighten, so that even in the dimness of the room they took on a silvery sheen. It was uncanny; almost as if he were experiencing some kind of revelation.

She waited expectantly. But he turned away and buttoned his shirt with quick, careful movements. Striding to the door, he half-opened it, then turned to face her.

'Care to go round the vineyards with me in the morning?' he asked.

She was startled. He had consistently refused to take her, and she wondered if his change of heart presaged a change of attitude. Was he seeing 'Mandy' as more than a pretty face and sexy body which he could pay off and dismiss from his mind? Could he be thinking in terms of a future with her? Of continuing as her

Svengali and grooming her to take her place beside him permanently? His face seconds ago had hinted at it, and she hid her exultation.

'I'd love to,' she replied sedately, and as he nodded and went out she bounded excitedly into the bathroom to put on her nightgown; then dashed back to bed, plumped up her pillows and lay back on them to build her castles in the air.

A soft tap at the door brought her quickly down to earth. It came again and her heart pounded. Had Piers returned to try his luck again? Switching on the bedside lamp, she reached for her dressing-gown, wrapped the satin folds firmly around her—she wasn't going to make it *that* easy for him—and hurried to the door.

'Who is it?'

Astonished, she heard Lucien's voice. 'May I speak to you, Mandy?'

'Can't it wait till morning?'

'I never seem to get you alone. Please, Mandy, let me in. I won't keep you long.'

Resignedly she turned the latch and motioned for him to come in. 'Well, what is it?' she asked, perching on the edge of her bed.

'I've come to apologise,' he said raggedly. 'Some of the things I said to you tonight and last weekend were unforgivable.'

She hadn't a clue what he was talking about, but as he appeared ready to cut his throat she knew he wouldn't appreciate her saying so.

'I—er—I've forgotten all about it,' she murmured.

'Which is exactly the answer a marvellous girl like you *would* give. But that still doesn't excuse my behaviour—offering to find you a job in Paris, when my sole motivation was to get you into bed.'

'You were only following the herd!' she said wryly.

'That's the last thing I want to do where you're concerned. Only I didn't realise it until tonight, when

I watched you dance with Piers. I love you, Mandy, and I want you to be my wife.'

'Your wife?' Amanda was too amazed to go on.

'Yes,' Lucien said eagerly. 'When this farce with you and Piers is over, I hope you'll stay in Paris and let me get to know you. I won't rush you, darling. I just don't want you walking out of my life.'

Amanda didn't know what to say. He looked as if he had gone through a hell of his own making since she had seen him downstairs. The urbane façade he presented to the world had been replaced by a dishevelled, vulnerable man spilling over with emotions he could not suppress. Somehow she liked him more this way, though she knew it could never turn into love. She was deeply upset she had hurt him. It had been stupid of her not to realise what was happening. But then, blinded by Piers, she had been blind to anyone else's feelings.

'I'm sorry, Lucien, but I . . . You'll always be a friend—a kind, dear friend—but nothing more.'

'How can you be sure? If we saw more of each other . . .'

'It would make no difference. Love isn't something you can turn on like a tap.'

'But it can grow,' he insisted. 'Don't turn me down out of hand.'

'I must. Forget me, Lucien.'

'I can't.' He leaned close and placed his lips gently on hers. But getting no response, he straightened. 'I'm sorry, Mandy. The last thing I want is to make a nuisance of myself. But just remember one thing. If you should ever need me, I'll always be there.'

Mutely, she nodded, and with tear-filled eyes watched him leave her room.

Alone again, she buried her head in her pillow. Her awareness of Lucien's hurt had taken the pleasure out of her magic moments with Piers, and she was unexpectedly afraid that she might have misread his behaviour. After all, offering to show her round the vineyards didn't constitute a proposal!

Yet surely it indicated a desire to change their relationship? She had thought so a few moments ago, and it was foolish to let Lucien's hurt make her doubt her judgment. Piers was in love with 'Mandy'. She was sure of it. But he was still scared by the differences between them.

With a deep sigh, Amanda sat up and wiped her eyes. It was time she dropped some of the less endearing mannerisms she had adopted, and became more her genuine self. No shrieking laughs, less 'ain'ts' and no more social gaffes. From tomorrow she would show him what a quick learner she was!

On this happier note, she snuggled down and went to sleep.

CHAPTER ELEVEN

AWAKE early next morning after a restless night, Amanda lay languidly thinking of Piers. The memory of his kiss was still vivid, and she ached to feel his arms round her.

But dwelling on it wasn't helping any, so she showered and dressed—easing herself into a pair of bottom-hugging turquoise trousers and matching top—then went downstairs for breakfast.

Piers was crossing the hall, and she gave him a warm smile and called out a cheerful 'Good morning.'

'It certainly is,' he called back, grinning. 'Join me for breakfast?'

'Love to.'

Together they entered the sunny, flower-filled room that opened off the terrace. It was here the family took their meals when there were no visitors, and, though it would have been considered large by normal standards, it was cosy and intimate compared with the rest of the château.

'How did you sleep?' Piers asked, pulling out her chair.

'Like a top. And you?'

'A restless top! My mind was spinning with all sorts of erotic images.'

'You should have tried a cold shower!'

'Even a freezing one wouldn't have helped!'

She laughed and helped herself to a freshly baked croissant. 'Then there's only one cure left.'

'I know.' He leaned towards her and winked. 'Maybe you'll help me find it tonight.'

The wink surprised her, and the fear that she meant no more to him than a one-night stand rose again to haunt her. All at once the sun lost its golden glow, the day its warmth, and she pushed away her croissant and settled for coffee, though it was all she could do not to pour it over his head!

Obliviously he munched his way through two brioches mounded with home-made apricot preserve, his air of nonchalance irritating her to the point of hysteria. Did he care nothing about the moments they had shared in her bedroom? Was she being stupid to think they had a future together?

'By the way,' he said casually, pouring himself a second cup of coffee, 'Lucien and Mariette asked me to say goodbye for them. They left at the crack of dawn—he was called back to Paris on business, and she's carrying on down to St Tropez.'

A plausible excuse, Amanda thought wryly, and wondered what Piers would say if she told him of Lucien's visit to her room. Yet there was no point in mentioning it, for she had no desire to cause a rift between the two friends.

'What's bugging you?' Piers asked cheerfully. 'You look about to blow a gasket.'

'Do I?' she feigned surprise.

He reached for another brioche. 'Look, Mandy, I hope you didn't get any ideas about last night?'

Amanda felt sick. So she was right. 'What do you mean by ideas?'

'About making this engagement of ours permanent.'

'Perish the thought,' she said promptly. 'As soon as you pay me, I'll be off. Today if you like.'

'Not quite so soon, my lovely. I'll need you for protection till I leave for California.'

'Won't you need protection there?' she enquired sarcastically. 'After all, with all those West Coast beauties lusting after you . . .'

'There's safety in numbers,' he chuckled. 'Anyway, women out there are far more relaxed about sex. They don't use it as marriage bait.'

Swallowing her anger, Amanda decided to try to catch him out.

'I still think you were crazy to use me as a cover when you've supposedly a perfectly good fiancée of your own.'

'There's no "supposedly" about it,' Piers stated. 'And as I've already told you, if my mother knew she'd insist I should tell Madame Le Blanc—which, for reasons you also know about, Hélène doesn't want me to do.'

'If she loved you, she'd want the whole world to know it.'

'She wishes to get her degree first,' Piers said stiltedly.

And you wish to go on lying, Amanda thought, remembering Lucien's comments about Piers and Hélène. Damn it, what man would refer to the woman he loved as 'a rose without scent'? It was a temptation to call his bluff, but she resisted.

'Anyway, why are we discussing Hélène?' Piers questioned. 'She's no concern of yours.'

Amanda shrugged, but her spirits rose again. The more he persisted with this fiction, the more certain she was that it was a defence against herself.

'Do you mind if we postpone the tour of the vineyards?' he went on, setting down his cup. 'I've a stack of work to catch up on.'

'Suits me,' she shrugged, saying no more as Madame Dubray came in and Piers pulled out a chair for her.

'You're up early, Maman.'

'I'm expecting Monique.' Madame Dubray gave Amanda a warm smile as she sat down.

'Monique?' Piers asked blankly.

'Yes, dear. Madame Le Blanc. She and Hélène drove down yesterday to meet their new tenants and go through the inventory with them. Then they're coming on here for a few days.'

Amanda was elated by the stony expression on Piers' face. His lie had come home to roost with a vengeance, and she couldn't wait to see how he extricated himself from what could be a very tricky situation.

'It will be like old times having them here,' Madame Dubray went on. 'Such a pity they moved away when Alphonse died.'

'What time are they due?' Piers asked in a strangled voice.

'This morning.'

'Then I'd better cancel my appointments for the day.'

Blue eyes flicked towards Amanda, but she pretended not to notice as he strode swiftly from the room.

Anxious not to give him an opportunity to contact Hélène and put her in the picture, she swallowed her coffee at a gulp and rushed after him.

He wasn't in his office or the library, and she was halfway upstairs—to see if he had gone to his room to telephone—when she heard his voice in the front driveway.

Dashing down again, she found him chatting to his estate manager. Guilelessly she strolled out and linked her arm through his.

'I'm talking business, Mandy. Why not go and sunbathe?'

'I'd rather be with you.' She rubbed her cheek against his shoulder, and from the corner of her eye saw the estate manager smiling at them benevolently.

The two men resumed their discussion and Amanda listened with interest, though she pretended not to understand a word. Finally the older man moved off, and Piers impatiently tried to pull free of Amanda's clinging hand.

'Look, Mandy, I've some urgent calls to make, so if you'll amuse yourself . . .'

Again he tried to ease his arm away but she hung on to it like a limpet. If he thought she was going to give him a chance to ring Hélène, he had another think coming!

But what came instead was a silver-grey Citroën, swinging sharply to a stop a few yards away and sending a spray of gravel flying.

Piers went stiff as a board, a dark tide of colour sweeping into his face. Amanda almost felt sorry for him as he walked jerkily towards the car.

'Wonderful to see you, Piers.' A buxom woman in a blue-grey dress, with hair to match, greeted him majestically as she stepped from the car. Above average in height, with a pouter-pigeon bosom, it was incredible she should be the mother of the dainty figure who followed her out. But she undoubtedly was, for Piers, side-stepping the bosom, greeted the girl with a kiss on each cheek.

'Dear Piers,' Hélène said liltingly, giving him her hands, which he raised to his lips.

Amanda tensed, then told herself not to be foolish. They had been neighbours for years and were bound to be on friendly terms. She stepped forward, and Piers flung her a tight look.

'This is Mandy, my fiancée,' he said perfunctorily, and before the two women could do more than smile at her, he turned towards the boot and lifted out their luggage.

Purposefully he led the way into the château, Madame Le Blanc marching beside him. But Hélène remained where she was, though she did not speak to Amanda until they were alone.

'Piers has told me so much about you,' she said with a friendly smile.

'Same here,' Amanda came back jauntily. 'Bet you were surprised to hear I'd nabbed him?'

'Why, no. He told me about it weeks ago.'

For the first time cold doubt shivered along

Amanda's spine. Had Piers been telling the truth after all? It was a devastating possibility, and Amanda, never one to beat about the bush, knew she had to find out.

She eyed the girl. It was easy to see why Piers had called her a 'rose', though she felt 'rosebud' would have been more apt, for the girl's heart-shaped face and soft dark eyes and hair gave her a virginal quality. But at a second glance there was a definite strength to be seen, for her mouth, though small, was firmly set, and her chin held more than a hint of stubbornness. Unbidden, a curl of apprehension spiralled through Amanda.

'Piers is such a slippery eel,' she made herself giggle, 'I won't rest easy till I've got him to the altar.'

'You don't need to pretend with me when we're alone,' came the gentle reprimand.

Amanda swallowed hard. So Lucien had got his wires crossed. Piers *was* engaged to Hélène! She wanted to scream, hit out, run away and hide. Yet she did none of these things, pride rooting her to the spot.

'You've gone awfully pale,' Hélène murmured. 'Are you feeling ill?'

'It's the heat.' With an effort Amanda pulled herself together. 'I must say you and Piers are a rum pair. I'm darned if I'd hide my love for someone simply because I had a bossy mother!'

'It has nothing to do with my mother,' Hélène confessed. 'I can easily stand up to her if I want to.'

'Then why——'

'Because I don't fancy settling down yet. Piers will be a demanding husband, but as a fiancé he's perfect.' The dark eyes sparkled mischievously. 'But for heaven's sake don't tell him any of this or he'll be furious.'

'I couldn't care less what you do,' Amanda shrugged. 'Though I think it's an odd way to behave.'

'Do you really? Personally I find the secrecy romantic and exciting.'

Hélène's tone, and the tinge of pink in her cheeks, told Amanda they were lovers, and she burned with jealousy. Yet what was one woman more in Piers' life? Did Hélène know the sort of man she was placing her trust in? For if he behaved so strangely at this juncture in their relationship, how would he act once they were married? Yet perhaps she was content to have part of him rather than nothing at all.

Amanda frowned. She would never be content with such a marriage. Anyway, it wouldn't arise, for she would have the subtlety to manipulate him, the courage to give him enough freedom to stop him from feeling tied, yet not so much that he would stray too far.

But first things first; and that meant removing Hélène from the scene. Funny, she felt no guilt at the thought. It went to show that, when love walked in through the window, conscience walked out of the door. But there was more to it than that. She had loved Piers the instant she had seen him—since a teenager, if truth be told—and, though it had taken her a while to admit it, she firmly believed their destinies were entwined.

'Why are you two still standing here?' Piers sauntered down the steps to rejoin them, and placed an affectionate arm round Hélène's shoulders. 'Put on your swimsuit and come down to the pool.'

'Lovely idea.' The girl turned with him towards the château. 'I haven't seen it since you had it installed, and I . . .'

Their voices faded as they disappeared through the massive stone portal, and Amanda—unwilling to follow after them like a puppy—gave them a chance to get ahead of her, before going up herself to change.

Anxious to be ensconced on a sun bed before the 'loving couple' joined her, she donned a bikini in record time, slipped on her Rayban sunglasses—excellent for hiding behind—and hurried down to the garden.

Though she had blithely assumed she'd have no trouble getting rid of Hélène, she was beginning to think otherwise, for, given that Piers' feelings for the girl mightn't run deep, he still saw her as a more suitable mother of his children than Mandy, with her humble background and dropped aitches.

Remembering how ruthlessly she had set out to infuriate and embarrass him, she didn't blame him for not seeing her as a permanent fixture in his life. Maybe if she had given in to him last night, he would have—but no, sex alone wouldn't make a man of Piers' disposition change the pattern he had mapped out for himself.

She slowed down and glowered at an innocent butterfly guzzling away at a crimson rose. Immediately the butterfly became Piers, the rose Hélène, the nectar . . . Oh, God! Amanda cried, this isn't a joke any more. I'm in far deeper than I thought, and if I can't make him love me . . . But she dared not dwell on that, for therein lay despair, and she wasn't a fighting Herbert for nothing.

Herbert! The name stopped her in her tracks. Piers might find difficulty in choosing between Hélène and Mandy, but what if it were Hélène and Amanda? Yet to come clean at this stage would negate the very reason why she had come here incognito. No, Piers must love her warts and all—even though the warts would be shed the instant he let his heart rule his head.

She reached the poolside: sparkling blue water, shimmering white marble surround hazy with heat, green and blue lounge beds. A sybarite's dream, though just now she was too immersed in gloomy thoughts to appreciate it.

Tossing her wrap on a slatted table, she settled

herself on a sun bed, her luscious curves barely
concealed by the two narrow strips of her black bikini.
As the heat beat down on her golden skin, her brain
whirled with one plan after another, and she had just
concluded that sunshine and birdsong were not
conducive to cohesive thought when a bell-like laugh
heralded the arrival of Piers and Hélène.

Through her dark glasses she watched them. His
curly black head was lowered to the girl's laughing
face, and hers was tilted to his, the better to see him,
giving Amanda the strong urge to put her hands round
the slender throat and squeeze!

Her ill-humour was not improved by seeing that
Hélène, petite though she was, was curvaceous in all
the right places, with breasts as pert as little apples,
their pointed nipples clearly visible through her scarlet
satin swimsuit.

Piers was also a sight worth watching. Though he
had been nude last night, the light had been too dim
for her to see him clearly. But the full light of day
revealed long powerful legs flecked with black hair and
a well-muscled chest with a mat of darker hair
tapering to a 'V' down the flat stomach and
disappearing into his minuscule briefs. Her pulses
hammered and she quickly turned her gaze to the calm
stretch of water.

But memory could not be so easily obliterated, and,
remembering his warm body upon hers last night, she
ached to touch it now, to stroke the roughened hair, to
feel the satiny skin against her breasts, her hands, her
mouth.

Another trill of laughter broke the spell, and she
gritted her teeth as she saw Hélène stretched out on a
bed close by, her hands entwined above her head,
making the bottom half of her bikini inch lower, where
the male eye was most guaranteed to go! And Piers'
certainly went, his blue gaze lingering as he settled
himself between the two girls.

The ham between the sandwich, Amanda thought gloomily, and the way he was smirking at Hélène was very hammy indeed!

Refusing to be drawn into small talk, she remained supine and silent, regarding the world through dark glasses that epitomised her mood.

'You could try being a bit more affable,' Piers hissed at her as Hélène wandered to the edge of the pool to dip her toe in the water.

'Why? She's *your* secret love, not mine.'

'Miaow, miaow! Jealous, are we?'

'Never of you!' Amanda snapped, forgetting her vow to be nice to him. 'Your threshold of excitement is too low for me, Piers. You'd go for anything with legs—even a piano!'

He chuckled. 'Is that why you're in such a foul mood?'

'Let's say I don't enjoy being a third wheel.'

'I didn't ask Hélène to come here. Their new tenants arrived a month early.'

'Really? I think she used it as an excuse to come and check up on you.'

'You mean you think she's jealous of *you*?' Piers laughed so heartily that Amanda's irritability turned to full-blown fury.

'Don't you think she'd have good reason if she'd seen you in my bedroom last night?'

He was completely unabashed by her remark. 'A man can love more than one woman.'

'Not "love",' Amanda snarled. 'The word you mean is "want". You've an eye like a roving satellite, and the staying power of a candle in the tropics!'

'I'll ignore the first comment,' he drawled, 'and deny the second!'

Amanda went scarlet, and Piers gave her a sharp smile. 'I'm glad you get my meaning.'

Casting a quick glance at Hélène, and seeing she still had her back to them, he feathered the tip of his finger along Amanda's bikini top, then deftly slipped his hand inside to caress the full curve. Instinctively her nipples stiffened, and, noting his appreciation of it, her love for him was swamped by despair.

'Don't you have any conscience?' she hissed, slithering away from his touch.

'I'm being true to myself, little Mandy. That's all my conscience requires.'

'And right now it requires me?'

'Don't you know?'

'I'm not sure I know anything where you're concerned,' she admitted soberly.

'Why not trust feminine intuition?'

'And if it lets me down?'

'I'll catch you.'

'And hold me?'

'Before letting you down *gently*,' he smiled, and, lithely rising, sauntered over to Hélène.

So much for *me*, Amanda thought, loathing his implication. Still, it was early days; she hadn't yet shown him the better side of her nature. Idly she watched him squat beside Hélène.

'Still nervous of going out of your depth?' she heard him tease.

The girl nodded, and before she could draw her feet out of the water he stopped her.

'Don't worry, *chérie*, only a fool would push you in. Put yourself in my hands for a few hours and I promise I'll have you ducking and diving before the session's over.'

'Using hypnotism?' Amanda called out scornfully.

Blue eyes met hers across the shimmering marble. 'When someone trusts you, you can get them to do most things.'

Amanda knew he was referring to last night, when she had lain in his arms and not dared let herself believe in his gentleness and coaxing. And how right she'd been!

Cheeks burning, she marched across to the diving board, climbed to the topmost level and executed a perfect somersault into the water. But she might as well have done a belly flop for all the notice she attracted, for Piers and Hélène were totally absorbed in one another.

Morosely, Amanda swam to and fro, occasionally doing the backstroke, occasionally the crawl. Watching the couple at the shallow end, she saw Hélène was genuinely scared of the water, and was surprised by Piers' patience with her. Well, at least he was not *all* bad! Only fickle and dishonest when it came to women!

Can I really tame him? she asked herself. Can we have a worthwhile marriage—assuming I can get him to the altar! Turning on her back, she floated, eyes shut against the sunlight. Logic told her to stick to her original plan of making Piers fall for her and then leaving him flat. Yet even as she considered this, she knew she couldn't walk away from him.

Aware of a rocking motion in the water, she lifted her head and saw him streaking towards her. Quickly she went into a racing crawl, but she was no match for him, and before she was halfway across the pool he had shot past her.

'Didn't I hear you tell Mariette you were only a fair swimmer?' he commented as she caught up with him under the diving board. '*I'd* call you a dark horse!'

'Neigh, sir,' she punned. 'I'd put my swimming on a par with my tennis.'

'Which means they're both first-rate. Where and when do you practise?'

'There are plenty of public swimming baths and tennis courts around.' She leaned against the side of the pool, not looking at him. Yet she was aware of the droplets glistening on his bulging forearms, and knew that brute strength alone would make him the winner in any contest between them. Physical contest only, though. Mentally, she'd give as good as she got.

'If you're as adept at indoor sports as outdoor ones,' he said softly, 'some man's going to be very lucky.'

'Can't you think of anything but sex?'

'Sure. But one always returns to what one enjoys most!' He folded his arms across his chest. 'Your trouble is that you're inhibited. A lusty love affair would do you the world of good.'

'I agree. That's why I'd like to get married!'

'How old-fashioned.'

Before she could think of a reply, a wild shriek sent them spinning round to see Hélène floundering in the water, arms flailing.

Within seconds Piers was at her side, lifting her out, and Amanda raced across to see if she could help.

'I warned you not to go out of your depth when I wasn't with you,' he was chiding.

'I know,' Hélène gasped, 'but I—I wanted to surprise you.'

'Frighten the wits out of me, you mean. Let *me* be your teacher, *chérie*, and decide how fast we proceed.'

Hélène shivered, and deftly he reached for his white towelling robe and wrapped it round her.

'Shall I get some coffee?' Amanda asked.

'I think something stronger is called for,' he said, and went behind the diving board to the rustic stone changing-rooms, which also housed a bar and sauna.

'How stupid of me,' Hélène apologised. 'But when I saw you and Piers swimming so well, I felt such an ass that——'

'You'll swim once you get confidence,' Amanda put in. 'And if anyone can give it you, Piers can.'

'I know. He's so tremendously assured. Even as a boy he knew what he wanted from life—and now he's got it.'

'With a title in the offing,' Amanda couldn't help saying.

'That's something he'd happily forgo,' Hélène answered. 'I can appreciate the Herberts wanting him for their daughter, but Piers is such a sensual man, it would never have worked out.'

'Apart from which he loves *you*,' Amanda said.

Padding footsteps brought their conversation to an end, as Piers returned with a bottle of Chablis in a cooler and three long-stemmed glasses.

'What shall we drink to?' he asked, pouring out the cool, greeny-gold liquid.

'To love,' Amanda said. 'It can hit you when you least expect it.'

'To sex,' Piers grinned, raising his glass. 'I *always* expect it!'

'To marriage,' Hélène added, 'which hopefully combines the two!'

'I'll certainly drink to that, my angel,' Piers took a long swallow, and Hélène caught Amanda's eye and spoke again.

'We French often speak prosaically about marriage, but we don't always mean what we say.'

'*You* do, *chérie*.' Piers feathered Hélène's cheek with his finger. 'That's what makes you special. My mother aside, you're the only honest woman I know.'

Amanda set down her glass with a snap that nearly broke its stem. She'd had enough! 'I think I'll go into Gerande and do some shopping,' she announced.

'Don't dash away on our account,' Piers said. 'If we want to be alone, we'll tell you.'

'It's better if we aren't alone, darling,' Hélène reminded him. 'You know how Mother watches me.'

'I wasn't going out of diplomacy,' Amanda grunted. 'I'm simply in the mood for spending money.'

'Take my car,' Piers suggested, then shook his head. 'Sorry. I doubt you could manage the Maserati.'

'I've driven one before,' Amanda said quickly, not relishing the prospect of a long wait for a local bus.

'And pigs fly!' he grinned. 'Gaston will take you there.'

'Don't you believe me?' she persisted.

'Oh sure. And you can drive a Rolls too!'

On the verge of saying she could, she hastily muttered, 'My boy friend's motorbike, actually.'

'Then Gaston will definitely drive you!'

It was noon when she reached the centre of the little market town, and the chauffeur arranged to wait for her in a cobbled side-street opposite a timber-faced inn where, he informed her, they served the best food in the district.

'I'll try it and tell you,' she promised, 'providing I can get a table.'

'M'sieur Piers has already booked one for you.' Gaston's smile revealed small, tobacco-stained teeth.

'M'sieur Piers anticipates everything,' she humphed, and, with no need to rush to book a place, decided to take a stroll.

It was already past noon and the shops were shut, so she could do little more than window-gaze. But she spotted two items she wanted to purchase: a bottle of plum liqueur for her father and a hand-painted sewing-box for her mother's embroidery silks.

A rumbling tummy finally drove her to the hostelry, where she lunched on pike fresh from the Loire, followed by a fresh salmon mousse spiked by tangy goat's cheese, the whole washed down with the glorious smoky flavour of a Pouilly Fumé, one of the district's most famed wines.

Only the knowledge that Piers and Hélène were together blighted her pleasure. Despite the girl saying that her mother watched them with eagle eyes, she still imagined them in each other's arms, and experienced such a sense of desolation that she couldn't bear to linger at the table.

Luckily the shops were now open, and she went to buy the two gifts she had seen, then, passing a mouth-watering cheese shop, was impelled to buy a basket of assorted cheeses for Madame Dubray.

The sun was painting the sky with dusky rose when she finally returned to the château. As she drove through the leafy gloaming, a strange sense of peace overtook her, making her far more sanguine about the future.

What Piers felt for spunky, warm-hearted 'Mandy' was too strong an emotion for him to turn his back on, especially after tonight, when she would show him a 'Mandy' he had never before seen.

CHAPTER TWELVE

IN a gracefully flowing flower-patterned voile that made her look as though she had stepped from a Gainsborough picture, Amanda made another of her startling entrances later that evening. That Piers was bemused by this new, softer version of 'Mandy' was evidenced by his expression, and, giving him a demure smile, she glided over to him.

'Miss me, darling?' she asked huskily.

'Every second.' The glint in his eye showed that he was in control of himself again, and she turned to Hélène and said graciously,

'Did Piers manage to get you back in the water this afternoon?'

'I'll say! And he worked a minor miracle. I can now put my head under water without being scared I'll drown!'

'Piers can teach anybody anything,' his mother said. 'It's a gift he has.'

'Well, he's certainly wonderful at teaching *someone* a lesson,' Hélène agreed, and the quickly masked laughter in her eyes as she glanced at him made Amanda wonder what secret joke they were sharing.

'A drink, Mandy?' Piers steered her none too gently towards the magnum of champagne reposing on a silver tray on the sideboard. 'You have an unusually revealing face,' he whispered. 'It's childish of you to be jealous of Hélène. You're wasting your time. I never was, and never will be your property.'

'Thank heavens for that,' Amanda muttered before she could stop herself. 'I was never one for living in a crowd!'

Accepting the drink he proffered, she turned her

back on him and took a wing chair opposite Hélène
and Madame Dubray, who were animatedly discussing
the preservation of historic houses; an apt subject,
since the girl was studying architecture. Watching her,
Amanda's high spirits sank to zero again. Hélène was
so suitable for Piers that she could not envisage him
giving her up for 'Mandy', no matter how drawn he
was to her.

She tried to imagine what she herself would do in
the same kind of situation—if she fell for a punk
rocker, for example. She would certainly resist it,
would probably even persuade herself it was physical
attraction and wouldn't last, which was probably what
Piers was doing at this precise moment!

Sitting up straight, and reverting to her more usual
spritely self, she clicked her fingers in his direction.
'Hey there! You ain't given me a refill yet.'

'Sorry.' He sauntered over with the champagne.

As he replenished her glass, he flashed Hélène an
intimate glance—as if reassuring her that she had
nothing to fear from this silly girl who was temporarily
in his life. Intercepting the look they exchanged,
Amanda was aware of the strong rapport between
them. Indeed, she had never seen Piers so relaxed, and
her despondency intensified. In an effort to overcome
it, she started chattering about her past life as a
parlour-maid, making it sound so colourful that
Madame Le Blanc listened open-mouthed.

'Mind you, it's not a job I'd recommend for a young
girl,' she concluded pertly. 'Some husbands are right
gropers behind their wives' backs!'

Piers spluttered into his glass, then in a strangled
voice suggested they went in to dinner, which
reminded Madame Dubray of the basket of cheeses
Amanda had bought her.

'It was a lovely thought, my dear. Thank you very
much.'

There was nothing patronising in the woman's tone,

and Amanda could have sworn that the smile in the dark eyes held affection. What a marvellous mother-in-law she would make, and what rotten luck if she couldn't be hers!

Yet the more she saw of Piers with Hélène, the less confident she became of her own chances. There was definitely a current of understanding between them, and it might be less painful for her to give up the fight here and now. So convinced was she of this as dinner progressed that she lost her appetite, and Piers, watching her push her food round her plate, asked what was wrong.

'I feel a bit queasy,' she lied. 'Too much wine at lunch, I guess. In fact, if you'll excuse me, I'll go to bed.'

'You'll find aspirins in your bathroom,' Madame Dubray said. 'But if you want something stronger——'

'No, thanks. Aspirins will do fine.'

Avoiding Piers' eyes, Amanda went out. Her sandalled feet made no sound on the carpeted stairs, nor did those of her pursuer, and she was startled to find Piers directly behind her as she reached her door.

'What do you want?' she asked, holding on to the handle.

'To talk to you.'

'We've done enough talking.'

Ignoring her, he pushed her into her room. 'I've told my mother we've broken our engagement,' he said baldly.

'*What?*'

'It's what you wanted me to do, wasn't it?'

'I wanted you to tell her the truth—that it was only a sham.' Amanda hoped he couldn't see she was trembling. 'Have you also told her you're going to marry Hélène?'

'Not yet. It will look better if I wait a few months.' He seated himself in an armchair beside the bed, one

long leg crossed over the other, looking very much at
home. 'This phoney engagement of ours has done me
a power of good with Hélène. She's finally agreed to
marry me before the year's out.'

Amanda's worst fears were confirmed, and her
trembling intensified. 'Looks like I deserve a bonus,
then,' she managed to say.

'No doubt of it. And it's one I hope you'll enjoy.'
He rose and came to her side, standing so close that
the special scent of him pervaded her nostrils.

'You're special to me, Mandy,' he went on, winding
a strand of her hair round his finger. 'You provoked
me and teased me and made my life hell, yet I can't
resist you any longer.'

'You can't?' she whispered, not sure she was hearing
correctly.

'No. Don't look so surprised, my love. You know
damn well what you do to me! I've never wanted
anyone as much as I want you, and I've no intention
of letting you out of my life.'

'But what about Hélène?' she gasped.

'My marrying her has nothing to do with *us*.'

'I—I don't understand.'

'It's simple, darling. I care for Hélène and she'll
make me an excellent wife. But you fulfil a part of me I
don't know existed until I met you.'

Amanda went on staring at him, too numb with
shock to feel pain. That would come later. For the
moment it was imperative not to let him know that his
insulting proposition had shattered all her dreams.

'So you want the two of us,' she whispered. 'Is that
it?'

'I wish it could be only you,' he said quickly, 'but it
wouldn't work. French society is far more rigid than
British, and you'd feel like a fish out of water.'

'Your mother's made me welcome,' Amanda
couldn't help saying.

'Because she's a kind and wonderful person. But . . .

well, she also feels marriage between us would be a disaster.'

'So it's Hélène to please society, and me to please yourself?'

The answer was on his face, and Amanda felt as though she were being squeezed in a vice. At last she was face to face with the real Piers: a rigid, hidebound man daring to offer second-best to the woman he loved, simply because she didn't fit into his social register. What an anachronism he was! It would have been ludicrous if it weren't tragic. Momentarily she shut her eyes, then opened them again to look into his. How blue they were, blue as the Madonna's robes, giving no hint of the devious mind that lay behind them.

'I love you, Mandy,' he said thickly, drawing her unresisting form into his arms, 'and we don't need a golden band to prove it. Let my body show you.'

His closeness turned her strength to putty, and she was powerless to move as the sweetness of his breath warmed her skin, and the hardness of his thighs gave truth to his words. His mouth found hers and her bones seemed to melt at its touch, though she could not respond to it.

After a moment he raised his head, puzzled. 'What's wrong, darling?'

'Everything. I always knew you had a rotten reputation with women, but I never thought you so despicable that you'd ... Oh, you're the most dishonest man I've ever met!'

'You can't mean that, Mandy.' He looked astounded. 'I've been totally honest with you.'

'And with Hélène too?'

'Not yet,' he conceded, avoiding her eyes. 'But she'll find out about us eventually, and she'll accept it.'

'What makes you so sure?'

'Because she's intelligent and practical. She wants a

socially acceptable marriage but a career too; so a husband who isn't too demanding will suit her admirably. Don't worry about it, my love, it will all work out.'

'For you, perhaps. Hélène and I are the ones who'll be shortchanged.'

'You'll never be short of anything, I promise you. I'll give you an apartment, clothes, money——'

'No!' she shouted. 'No!'

Drawing a shuddering breath, she knew she had to get out of this situation with her pride intact. But how? Her mind raced, one idea after another tumbling through it, only to be discarded. Yet she had to say something—anything—to hide her humiliation.

'It's no use,' she mumbled, grasping at the one idea that seemed feasible. 'I can't go on hiding it.'

'Hiding what?'

'The truth. You're an attractive man, Piers, and it's been fun flirting with you. But . . . well, to be honest, Lucien's asked me to marry him, and I'm going to accept.'

From the rush of colour that suffused Piers' face, Amanda knew she had given him a shock. But only to his ego, for he wasn't capable of love.

'Cat got your tongue?' she asked with forced flippancy. 'Or did you think you were the only man who thought me worth having?'

'I certainly didn't think in terms of you and Lucien. I never guessed he was serious about you.'

'Goes to show how wrong you were. I may not be good enough to be *your* wife, but Lucien thinks I'm good enough to be *his*.'

'But you haven't said yes, have you?' Piers questioned sharply. 'You just told me you're *going* to accept.'

How astute he was! Well, so was she. 'There are certain things about myself that I'd like him to know first,' she said carefully, 'and I didn't want to tell him until I'd left here.'

'What things?'

'They're only of concern to the man I marry.'

'And that's going to be Lucien?' Piers asked sarcastically. 'It's a good try, Mandy, but somehow I don't believe you. I think you're saying it because you feel I've insulted you.'

'Well, I can't say I was flattered by your offer. But I assure you it has nothing to do with my feelings for Lucien.'

A narrowed blue gaze raked her face, and with all the strength of pride she could muster she made herself look him in the eye. He was the first to turn away, his expression shuttered.

'You really love him, then?' Piers' voice was stilted, as if he found speaking an effort.

'Yes,' she lied.

The colour, that was still high in his face, seeped away, giving his tan a greyish tinge. 'Then it was fortunate you came to France. If it weren't for our charade, you wouldn't have met him.'

'I know. And I'll always be grateful to you.' Amanda marvelled she could continue to lie with such ease. But then, she'd been doing little else since she had spoken to Piers from her bedroom window, and it seemed appropriate that their parting should end on a lie too.

'Yes, I'm grateful to you,' she reiterated, 'and because of it I won't take the money you agreed to pay me.'

'Look on it as a wedding present,' he jibed.

'I won't need it.'

'No, I don't suppose you will.'

His voice was still as cold as his expression. How different he looked from the confident man who'd come into her room a few moments ago. Was it because he genuinely cared for 'Mandy'? Yet, if so, how could he marry Hélène? Anger and disgust kept her tears at bay, though the bitterness of it clogged her throat.

'I think it's best if I leave in the morning, Piers.'

'I agree.' He hesitated, as though he wished to say more. Then his lips set together and he went out, shutting the door quietly behind him, shutting it too on all her hopes.

So deep was her misery that Amanda could not cry, and undressing shakily she crept into bed. But her thoughts remained with Piers, in his room at the other end of the corridor.

What would he have said if she had confessed to being Amanda Herbert? Would he have consigned Hélène to limbo and embraced a future with a girl who could be both wife and mistress to him? After all, what more could a man ask? Miserable as she was, Amanda could not help a wry smile, though it soon turned to tears, which coursed hotly down her cheeks. She had gambled on Piers offering marriage, and had lost. But at least her pride was intact, thanks to Lucien.

With a gasp she sat upright. Lucien! She must speak to him before Piers did, otherwise he might admit she'd turned him down!

Quickly she dialled Enquiry for his home number, and within a moment heard his voice on the line.

'It's Mandy here,' she said breathlessly. 'I—er—I just thought I'd let you know I'm leaving here tomorrow and—and if you like I'll stop over in Paris to see you.'

'If I like? It's what I want more than anything else! But what's with you and Piers?'

'The job's finished. I'll tell you about it when I see you.'

'What time are you arriving?'

'I'm not sure. I'll call you when I get in.'

'You'll stay with me, of course.'

'No, thanks. I'll book into a hotel.'

'There's no need. You can trust me, Mandy. I mean it.'

'Right now you do!'

'Little cynic!' he chuckled. 'Well, at least let me meet you at the station and—damn, I can't. I'll be tied up at a meeting all day and won't be free till six.'

'Then I'll come to your apartment. Expect me around seven.' Before he could argue she replaced the receiver.

Even as she did, she regretted using him as a cover, knowing how much simpler it would have been had she told Piers she was in love with someone in England. But it was too late now. She had embarked on another charade, and had to see it through.

CHAPTER THIRTEEN

A SLEEPLESS night sent Amanda into the breakfast-room early next morning, and she was surprised to find Madame Dubray already there. Wishing she had had the foresight to skip the meal, Amanda mumbled 'good morning' and took her place at the table.

'I understand you're leaving us,' Madame Dubray said, coming straight to the point.

'Yes.'

'I must say I'm surprised. I thought you cared for my son, and now I find you and Lucien . . .'

Trust Piers to put the blame on *me*, Amanda fumed. He must have rushed back to his mother to whitewash himself!

'We—er—d-didn't want it to happen,' she stammered. 'It just did!'

'Did it?' Seeing Amanda's puzzlement, Madame Dubray went on, 'I wondered whether you were simply paying Piers back for the way he concentrated on Hélène?'

'Piers' behaviour has nothing to do with my loving Lucien,' Amanda stated, more furious than ever that he hadn't told his mother the whole truth. 'And I can't believe you really mind me pushing off. Your son and I are poles apart.' Gulping down her coffee, she stood up. 'Do you have a train timetable to Paris? I'd like to leave as soon as possible.'

'Gaston will drive you there.'

'I'd rather he didn't.'

'Piers insisted,' Madame Dubray said. 'He also asked me to apologise for his absence, but he was called urgently to one of the vineyards.'

'It doesn't matter,' Amanda shrugged. 'We've no

more to say to each other. But please say goodbye to
Hélène for me.'

'Of course. You only missed her by a few moments.
She went off to join Piers.'

All too easily Amanda pictured the girl walking
beside him through the green vines, and as she went to
her room to pack she could barely keep her eyes from
staring out of the window towards the distant slopes.
Let Hélène have him! She pitied anyone who tied their
life to his.

Feverishly she filled her cases, and only as she went
to shut the first one did she stop. Why was she taking
these things? She wanted nothing from Piers, no
reminder of him continually to hurt her. Dumping the
entire contents on the bed, she picked up her purse
and walked out.

Some four hours later, the chauffeur-driven
Maserati entered the busy streets of Paris, with its one
forlorn passenger.

'*The last time I saw Paris my heart was young and
gay.*' The Oscar Hammerstein lyric resounded in
Amanda's head. '*I heard the laughter of my heart in
every street café!*'

But now all she heard were sighs from the heart,
and as they cruised down the Champs Elysées, tears
blurred the leafy foliage of the trees into a green mist.

'Where do you wish me to take you?' Gaston asked,
and she gave him the address of the small, exclusive
hotel where her parents always stayed.

Only as they turned into a cobbled yard off the
Avenue Foch and Amanda saw the St Léonard and
was welcomed as a friend by Madame Maury, the
proprietress, did she begin to re-establish her own
persona, and in so doing start to see the past few weeks
and Piers with a greater sense of detachment. It did
not minimise her heartbreak, but it helped her to
accept it.

Kisses on each cheek were exchanged, and Madame

herself escorted Amanda to the second floor and an elegantly furnished suite.

'Is your luggage being sent?' Madame Maury enquired, and Amanda nodded, reluctant to admit she didn't have any.

With a smile, the woman left, and Amanda debated whether to ring her mother and tell her she was no longer at the château. Yet she was in no mood for 'I told you so's', and instead decided to do what every intelligent young woman should do in the circumstances: buy herself some new clothes!

For the next few hours she shopped madly, trying to forget the last time she had done so, with Piers. Today she gave rein to her own taste, and with unaccustomed extravagance bought several outfits before going on to Carita to have her ghastly orange hair changed back to its original auburn.

It was marvellous to look her own self again, and in considerably lifted spirits she returned to the hotel to change for her meeting with Lucien.

She decided on a flowing emerald-and-white dress that skimmed her curves yet subtly defined them, topping it with a wide-shouldered jacket checked in the same colours. It was a dramatic outfit, but she had the panache to carry it off, as she did the sophisticated hairstyle that had been created for her a few hours earlier: auburn tresses piled atop her head to show her slender neck and highlight her classic profile. Her make-up was discreet and her skin glowed with its own natural bloom. Almost the old Amanda, she mused as she descended to a waiting cab. Almost, but not quite. The sparkle in her eyes and the joy in her heart were missing.

Lucien lived on the top floor of a centuries' old house overlooking the Seine, in one of Paris's most prestigious residential areas, and as she emerged from the ancient lift he was waiting in the entrance hall to greet her, a manservant hovering behind him.

Unlike Piers' apartment, which had been filled with antiques, this one was a modern bachelor pad, with stark colours, floor sculptures and hard-edge paintings, all redeemed—in Amanda's eyes—by shelves filled with books, and a massive collection of classical records. No ordinary man about town this, she decided, but one with unexpected depths. Not quite so unexpected, though, for from the start Lucien had shown her a sympathy and understanding Piers didn't have. Yet it was Piers she loved, Piers for whom her body craved.

'It's wonderful having you here,' Lucien said earnestly.

In impeccably cut beige suit, with cream shirt and discreet tie, he looked far different from the casually garbed man who weekended in the country. Certainly not a man to treat lightly, and definitely not one to deceive.

Amanda's guilt grew, and, thinking of the deception she was about to enter, knew she could not hurt Lucien by going through with it. She would tell him her identity and then leave.

'You turned me down so flatly the other night,' he went on, 'I'd given up all hope of seeing you again.'

'I couldn't come to Paris and *not* see you,' she hedged.

His eyes devoured her, moving from her face to her tall, curvaceous body and long, slim legs. The rays of the setting sun bounced off the edge of the windowpane to burnish her hair lightly, and a puzzled look came into his eyes. He went to speak, then with a shake of his head led her to a chair.

Giving him full marks for self-control—he obviously couldn't quite make out what was different about her—an imp of mischief prompted her to play the waiting game, and see how long it took him to recognise that the change in her came from more than outward trappings.

'How about some champagne?' he asked.

'Lovely. But dry, please.'

'I've some Pol Roger——'

'Too much body for my taste,' she cut in, barely managing to keep a straight face as his mouth fell open. 'Do you have any Heidsieck?'

'As a matter of fact I do. But it's rather dry and I——'

'Wonderful,' she beamed, stifling her laughter as she watched him disappear into the kitchen.

He returned a moment later with the champagne in an ice bucket and two narrow, fluted glasses.

'Heavenly,' Amanda breathed, accepting a glass and holding it to her nose. 'Beats me how anyone can use a swizzle stick.'

'A swizzle stick?'

'To stir out the bubbles. Desecration, don't you think?'

'Er—yes, quite,' Lucien said.

'After all, it's the bubbles that make champagne so elevating. But I'm sure you know that.'

'Yes, of course. But I didn't think *you* did.'

Hiding another smile, she crossed her legs in ladylike fashion at the ankles, and watched him through her lashes, amused by his growing bewilderment.

'How come you left the château so suddenly?' he asked.

'Because of Hélène.'

'Hélène Le Blanc? I don't understand.'

'She was staying there with her mother for a few days, and it brought things to a head. She and Piers have been secretly engaged for months.'

'You're joking!'

'I'm not.'

'And he never told me?' Lucien was amazed. 'The sly devil!'

'His mother doesn't know yet either,' Amanda

added. 'But I gather he intends marrying before the year's out.'

'He's certainly played his cards close to his chest.' Lucien was still bewildered. 'All his talk of not getting married for years, when all the time he and Hélène . . . Just wait till I see him!'

Wisely, Amanda remained silent. She felt Lucien eyeing her, and was not surprised when he set down his glass and came to stand in front of her.

'Something's happened to you, Mandy. Not only have your looks changed, but so has your accent.'

'Really?' she drawled, tilting back her head to look at him, her wide grey eyes ingenuous. 'Do you like the new me?'

'Of course, but I liked the old one too. In fact it was the old Mandy I proposed to, if you remember?'

'How can I forget?' she said huskily, and, still hurting from Piers, lifted her hands towards Lucien.

He took them, and seating himself beside her, studied her carefully.

'That dress has far more flair than the others I've seen you wear, and your make-up's different too. But it's more than that. There's a—aah, I've got it! You've changed the colour of your hair!'

'From spring carrot to autumn pomegranate!' she said.

He chuckled. 'The quick wit hasn't changed, though, Mandy my love.'

'Amanda,' she said, taking the bull by the horns. 'Amanda Herbert.'

'I assumed Amanda was your full name . . .' Lucien's voice trailed away. 'Did you say *Herbert*?'

'That's right. Amanda Diana Catherine Herbert, of Herbert House.' She jumped up and went to stand by the window, knowing it would be easier to explain herself if she kept her distance.

'This seems to be my day for shocks,' Lucien said. 'I suppose there was a reason for your masquerade?'

'It began as a joke,' she confessed. 'But it will be easier if I start from the beginning.'

Haltingly she did, telling him everything except her love for Piers.

'What a brilliant joke!' Lucien chuckled as she came to the end. 'And you carried it off superlatively. Mind, there were times when I thought you were a split personality! Several things about you didn't add up, but that you should be Amanda Herbert . . .' He shook his head. 'And Piers doesn't know?'

'He hasn't a clue!'

'I shouldn't think any man has, where you're concerned!' Purposefully Lucien came towards her. 'I can see why you sent me packing the other night. There you were, kidding Piers along, and there was I, bleating on about teaching you everything you wanted to know. Lord! what a laugh you must have had!'

The raw emotion in his voice reinforced her conviction that it was wrong to use him as a shield against Piers. Nothing could excuse her hurting this charming, most gentle of men.

'Lucien, I——'

The insistent peal of a bell stopped her, and it was followed almost instantly by a deep, melodious voice in the hall, a voice that sent shock waves reverberating through her. What was Piers doing here? Fighting to control her nerves, she watched him stride in—emanating a repressed impatience that filled the air with an electric charge.

'Sorry to barge in on you, Lucien,' he began, then stopped abruptly as he saw Amanda at the window. 'So you're here?' His voice was hard, angry almost.

'Where else did you expect me to be?' she countered, gathering together the broken shards of her pride.

'You've been played for a fool, old man,' Lucien grinned.

'A fool?'

'Without question. Take a look at Mandy. Isn't she different?'

'From what?'

'The buck-toothed vision who waved to you from the window at Herbert House?' Lucien's smile turned to laughter as he saw Piers' eyes narrow.

'You mean Amanda and—and——'

'Mandy are one and the same,' Lucien finished for him, waving his hand towards her. 'Meet Mandy Jones, otherwise known as Amanda Herbert.'

'And soon to be Amanda Delon,' she added, and, seeing Lucien's face, could have kicked herself. How could she have allowed her desire to anger Piers to lead her into a situation that would also hurt Lucien? But it was too late to draw back what she had said, and with forced jauntiness she walked towards him and linked her arm through his.

'Dearest,' Lucien breathed, and she quickly put her fingers upon his mouth, her eyes sliding to Piers, who was watching them with a stony expression.

'You've undoubtedly hit the jackpot, Lucien,' Piers drawled. 'You propose to the maid and end up with the mistress!'

Preferable to being *your* mistress! Amanda thought bitterly, but knew better than to say so, for if Lucien learned of Piers' insulting proposition it would put paid to their friendship. And since she had no intention of marrying Lucien—dear Lord, how two-faced she was being to him—she did not want to come between them. If only Piers had not arrived tonight and forced her hand. Yet instinct told her he had deliberately called here to check her story.

'I hope you aren't cross with me for my masquerade?' she asked him with a smile. 'But you played right into my hands that day in the woods.'

'I see that now.' His tone was mild, though his mouth was a hard line.

'And you forgive me?'

'Of course.'

'So all's well that ends well,' Lucien added. 'And now I suggest we drink a toast to our engagement.'

'Yours too,' Amanda said to Piers. 'I told Lucien. I hope you don't mind?'

'Not at all. It's no longer a secret, anyway. We told our respective mothers at lunchtime, and it's all official and duly blessed!'

'Is Hélène in Paris with you?' Amanda was amazed she could speak when her mouth seemed full of bitter ashes.

'Yes. Even the sanest female seems to go crazy over clothes when marriage looms, and she won't name the day until she finds out when St Laurent can make her wedding dress!'

'Why don't we all go out tonight and celebrate?' Lucien suggested.

'Hélène and I are dining with her aunt and uncle.'

'Families!' Lucien grinned, and caught Amanda's hand. 'I can't wait for mine to meet you. But my parents are in the States for the next three months.'

Thanks heavens for small mercies, Amanda thought. It was bad enough deceiving Lucien, let alone his mother and father.

'But that won't prevent me from meeting yours again,' he went on. 'I daresay your father will want to have a chat with me.'

'I wouldn't worry about it,' Amanda smiled. 'Any friend of Piers comes with an immediate sign of approval.'

'Hear that?' Lucien teased his friend. 'At last I've discovered the benefit of knowing you!'

'Without me you wouldn't have known Amanda either,' came the comment.

'For which I'm doubly grateful.' Lucien drew Amanda's hand to his lips, and it was all she could do not to pull it away.

'I'll leave you two lovebirds,' Piers said abruptly, setting down his glass.

'Did you have any special reason for calling?' she heard Lucien ask as he accompanied Piers to the door.

'You wanted my shirtmaker's address in Hong Kong, remember? I was going to phone it through, but as I was passing I thought I'd drop in and tell you about Hélène at the same time.'

'I'm delighted you did. Quite something, eh? Two dyed-in-the-wool bachelors getting hooked at the same time!'

'Some are more hooked than others,' Amanda said, sauntering into the hallway, and saw from the jut of Piers' jaw that her barb had hit home. What price his love for Hélène when it hadn't stopped him asking another girl to share his bed?

'So what's your shirtmaker's address, then?' Lucien asked, taking a notebook from his breast pocket and searching in his others. 'Damn! I've mislaid my pen.'

'Would this be it?' Piers asked, withdrawing a narrow gold one from his pocket.

'How come *you've* got it?' Lucien exclaimed.

'It was found in Mandy's—in Amanda's room,' came the expressionless reply.

Pink-cheeked, Amanda looked away. Not so Lucien.

'I must have dropped it when I popped in on her to pop the question! Now what's that address?'

In a dry voice Piers gave it to him, then opened the door.

'Remember me to Hélène,' Amanda called.

'Will do,' he said, and with a nonchalant wave was gone.

Instantly Lucien pulled Amanda close. 'I still can't believe you've agreed to marry me, darling. What made you change your mind?'

'It's a woman's prerogative,' she teased, easing slightly back from him. 'But a liberated one mightn't appeal to you so much.'

'Everything about you appeals to me.'

'Don't be so sure. I've very strong opinions and I'll never let any man order me around.'

'That's par for the course, these days,' he smiled, 'and we poor men accept it.'

'Piers doesn't.'

'Yes, he does. You don't know him as well as I do, darling. Admittedly he gave you a hard time, but then you rather asked for it! When I think of the outrageous things you said and did . . .' He began to laugh. 'You must have stayed up at night working out how to aggravate him!'

'Can't we stop talking about Piers?' she said impatiently.

'By all means.' He led her into the sitting room and drew her down on to a settee. 'You've told me a lot about Mandy—all fiction, I suppose?—but I know very little about Amanda.'

'There's not much to tell. I'm a freelance journalist and I often go abroad on assignments. Sometimes for months,' she lied, seeing this as her eventual way of parting from him.

'That'll make our time together all the sweeter,' Lucien murmured, tracing the curve of her cheek with his hand.

'You might get irritated if I'm away too often,' she warned.

'Why are you being so negative, darling?' He pulled her close again. 'If we love each other, we can work through *any* problems.'

Problem was she *didn't* love him, and she was more convinced of it than ever as his hands slid down her back to her waist, then lower still to press her thighs upon his.

'Darling,' he breathed heavily, and expertly prised her lips apart.

When it came to kissing, he was no slouch. But then she hadn't expected him to be. What she hadn't

expected was the rage he aroused in her; an insane
desire to tear away his hands and run. With an
enormous effort she remained passive.

Too passive, it seemed, for Lucien lifted his face
away from hers, his sherry-brown eyes quizzical.

'You talk of love, Amanda, but you don't act
loving.'

'I'm sorry,' she whispered. 'I guess I need time to
get my head together. I haven't been Amanda Herbert
for so long I seem to have lost myself.'

'Poor darling.' He tilted up her face and stroked the
petal-soft skin. 'You need to go home, I think, and put
your roots into your own earth.'

It was a shrewd comment, and her respect for him
grew. She sighed, wishing respect could grow into love.

'On the other hand, there may be another
explanation,' he went on, humour in his voice. 'You've
had a long day, and I bet you've eaten nothing since
breakfast!'

'Not even that,' she smiled.

'Then let's satisfy the physical appetite before the
sexual!'

Startled, she sat up straight. 'I'm not going to bed
with you, Lucien, if that's what you're saying.'

'Hoping's more the word, darling. But I won't rush
you.'

'I'm glad to hear it,' she said drily and, jumping to
her feet, went over to a mirror to tidy her hair. 'I think
I'll go home tomorrow.'

'Won't you at least stay the weekend? I promise not
to pressurise you.'

Aware that if she left Paris too quickly it might
arouse Piers' suspicion, she had no alternative but to
agree, and, seeing Lucien's face light up, determined
to end the engagement as soon as she feasibly dared.

'You're far too nice for me,' she murmured.

'Little fool,' he said gruffly. 'Don't you know it's
easy to be nice to someone you love?'

She nodded, knowing how easy it would have been for her to be nice to Piers. But he belonged to Hélène—and to any other woman who caught his roving eye.

If only he would go to California! Only when he was on the other side of the world would she stand a chance of getting on with her own life.

CHAPTER FOURTEEN

LEANING back in the seat of the plane winging its way to London, Amanda put on her sunglasses, much to the amusement of the man beside her.

'There's no sun in here, lady,' he said with a Canadian twang.

She smiled wanly and turned away, knowing he hadn't said a truer word, and hoping the deep-tinted lenses would hide the tears that kept welling into her eyes. Indeed, it had been an effort hiding them from Lucien, who had insisted on driving her to Charles de Gaulle Airport earlier that afternoon.

He had been deeply disappointed that she had changed her mind about remaining for the weekend, though she had tried to convince him that only an emergency had made her do so.

'Liz—the editor I mostly write for—called my mother and said she needs an article from me urgently,' she lied. 'Someone's let her down, and she's faced with three blank pages.'

'Don't magazines keep articles in reserve?' Lucien had grumbled. 'Seems to me you can't wait to go.'

'Don't be silly. Anyway, you'll be coming over next weekend.'

'If you don't call and say you've been sent to the moon!' He sighed. 'When I awoke this morning, I was half afraid yesterday had been a dream. I'd planned to take today off and——'

'I warned you I took my work seriously,' she cut in. 'If you can't accept that . . .'

'Of course I accept it. It's simply that I'd counted on having a few days alone with you.'

Feeling a deceitful coward, Amanda had kissed him

goodbye and hurried through Customs, only coming to herself as the aircraft had lifted from French soil.

Leaving Heathrow by taxi an hour later, she could not help thinking how much she had changed from the carefree young woman who had travelled this motorway a few weeks ago with Piers. Now, with every mile bringing her nearer Herbert House, she was filled with apprehension, knowing she not only had her own misery to contend with but her parents' disappointment that she and Piers hadn't hit it off.

Yet, despite this, her spirits rose as the taxi pulled up outside the ivy-covered façade of her beloved home, and she saw her mother and father hurrying down the steps to welcome her.

'Wonderful to have you back, my dear,' her father boomed, in the tone he adopted when speaking to foreigners or beset by emotion. 'Good thing I wasn't told about the trick you intended playing on Piers, or I'd have put a stop to it. Must have been furious when he found out, eh?'

Amanda shook her head and gave her father a hug. Come to think of it, Piers had said remarkably little. But then, his fury that she'd turned him down in preference to Lucien had probably blotted out every other emotion.

'Such a pity things didn't work out between the two of you,' her mother murmured.

'There was never any chance of that. He's just got himself engaged to Hélène Le Blanc. Her family own the property next to the château. She's a very sweet girl.'

'You've met her?'

'Oh yes. She and her mother spent last weekend with us. Look, I know you're disappointed,' she went on, following them both into the library, 'but, as I said, it didn't gel between us.'

'Then that's that,' her mother replied. 'Your happiness is all that counts with us. Now sit down and tell us the whole story. Knowing you, you must have pulled Piers' leg dreadfully!'

'Both legs!' Amanda laughed, hoping her gaiety didn't sound forced, and immediately launched into a censored version of the past weeks' events, for even her mother would draw the line at some of the outrageous pranks to which she'd subjected Piers.

'You made him buy the *largest* bottle of "Joy",' her mother tried to look aghast, but spoiled it by crumpling into laughter. 'Amanda, how *could* you!'

'Quite easily. If every sneer and command he gave me had been a drop of scent, I'd have ended up with a gallon! You can't imagine how awful he——' Amanda stopped mid-sentence as the housekeeper came in with an enormous bouquet of long-stemmed tea roses.

'For you, Lady Amanda,' she said. 'They just arrived.'

With trembling hands, Amanda reached for the card nestling among the blooms.

'From Piers?' her mother asked as the housekeeper went out.

'From Lucien, his friend. I—er—we saw quite a bit of each other while I was away.'

'From the size of the bouquet,' her father humphed, 'looks as if he'd like to see a whole lot more!'

Amanda, aware of the look that passed between her parents, knew she had to come clean about him. At least as clean as she dared! 'As a matter of fact I've invited him here next weekend.'

'How nice,' her mother murmured. 'I only vaguely remember him. Not quite as tall as Piers, I think.'

'A five-foot-eleven-inch dwarf,' Amanda said, straightfaced, and saw her father grin.

'Is he serious about you?' he asked.

'Serious enough to want to marry me.'

There was a startled silence.

'And how do *you* feel?'

Amanda hesitated. She was in no mood to confide

her true emotions to anyone, and reluctantly knew that, like it or not, she still had to use Lucien to protect herself. 'I've—er—said yes.'

'Rather precipitate, isn't it?' her mother commented.

'I suppose so. I—er—we haven't set a date for the wedding yet.'

'Very wise of you,' her father stated, and, muttering that he wanted to walk the dogs, went out.

'Piers must have been amused by the turn of events,' her mother said. 'He probably considers himself a matchmaker!'

'I think he was taken by surprise.'

'As *we* were. But as long as you're happy . . .'

'I am, Ma.'

'You don't look it.'

'I'm tired, that's all. So stop fishing.'

Margaret Herbert picked up the petit point embroidery she was working on and carefully made a stitch. 'Two wrongs won't make a right, you know.'

'What's that supposed to mean?'

'That rushing from one situation into another is not always the best solution.'

'Ever considered taking up psychology?' Amanda quipped.

'Mothers do it automatically,' came the blithe retort. 'And remember, I'm always here if you want to talk to me.'

'We're talking now, for heaven's sake!'

'Surface chat, my dear. When you're ready for something deeper, I promise you a sympathetic ear and a closed mouth!'

Tears, still near the surface, blurred Amanda's vision. 'Thanks, Ma. I'll take a raincheck on that. And now I must go through my mail.'

'It's on the desk in your room, with some telephone messages. Liz Burton from 'Modern Girl' rang twice yesterday. Says she has a job for you.'

Amanda was delighted. At least one of her lies had come true! 'Great,' she said. 'Writing's the one thing I missed most these past weeks.'

But once in her room she was in no hurry to return Liz's call. Curling up on the window seat, she stared down into the rose garden, wishing she was once again the light-hearted girl who, with orange feathers from a duster and face spotted with lipstick, had play-acted the joke that had so surprisingly backfired on her.

A red setter loped excitedly across the lawn, followed at a sedater pace by her father. The sight of him brought the distant future into focus, reminding her that one day she would have to face the prospect of Piers taking up partial residence here with Hélène. Painfully she envisaged dark-haired little boys with jewel-blue eyes and curly black hair, children she would have given ten years of her life to mother. But it was not to be, and she must plan a different future.

It was this that set her dialling Liz's number to say she was coming to London next day. The quicker she applied herself to work, the less time there would be for thinking. The months ahead were going to be rough, no use denying it, but she had the strength of character to win through.

'So where are you sending me this time?' she asked her friend as she breezed into her office on the top floor of a skyscraper overlooking Waterloo Bridge.

'South America. I want a pithy series on the lifestyles of the women there, with the accent on social issues rather than high society.'

'Getting serious in our old age, are we?'

'Definitely. I had a bust-up with my chairman last week, and said I'd resign if I had to publish any more articles on pop stars and their lovers, or soap opera wardrobes!'

'Good for you. It'll be fun getting my teeth into something worthwhile for a change.'

'Not *someone*?' Liz raised a carefully pencilled eyebrow.

'Stop being nosy.'

'Not nosy, my angel, simply madly interested. You disappear for weeks on end, then surface again, pounds thinner and haunted-looking as Camille—which means there's a man lurking in the background!'

'And in the background is where he'll stay,' Amanda retorted.

'Don't you trust my discretion?'

'No!'

Liz grinned. 'Okay, let's stick to business. I'll get your itinerary worked out and call you. But be ready to leave in three weeks.'

Amanda wished it could have been sooner, not relishing the prospect of coping with an ardent Lucien this long. Besides, every time they met she would be reminded of Piers, and the dull ache that was a perpetual part of her life would become a throbbing pain.

Yet, surprisingly, Lucien's presence at the weekend had the opposite effect. There was no greater balm to a woman's bruised ego, she decided, than being pandered to by a handsome, intelligent and amusing man.

Away from Piers' commanding presence, his quieter one came into its own, and he discussed estate management with her father, offered helpful advice on interior decoration to her mother—having confessed that his maternal aunt was a world-renowned interior designer—and charmingly made no secret of his deep affection for their daughter. Yet despite his attributes he wasn't Piers, and failed to touch the inner core of Amanda's being, to ignite the spark that would put stars in her eyes, bring a tremble to her limbs.

'Come to any decision about us yet?' he asked her

on the Sunday afternoon, as they waited on the terrace for the car that was to take him to the airport.

'Decision about what?'

'Our marriage.'

Her heart thumped painfully. 'We've just got engaged. I don't want to rush things.'

'Unlike me,' he sighed. 'I'd marry you tomorrow. You bowled me over the night you walked into that restaurant in Paris with Piers.'

'As far back as then?'

'First sight, first love. When I watched the spunky way you stood up to Piers, I could have cheered.'

Amanda laughed. 'I guess I was a better actress than I thought.'

'Was it *all* an act?'

A note in his voice put her on guard. 'Depends what you mean by "*all*".'

'Your jealousy of Yvonne—the girl you spilt coffee over—and the way you gave Mariette her come-uppance. Seemed she really got to you.'

'I was never jealous of Mariette,' Amanda stated carefully. 'I didn't like her as a person, which was why I gave her a rough ride. So if you think I'm hiding a secret passion for Piers—forget it.'

'What about his feelings for you? I know him too well to believe he'd see a beautiful girl and not try to bed her!'

'Aren't you forgetting Hélène?' Lucien's startled expression told her he had, and she pressed home the advantage. 'To Piers, I was simply someone who could help him out of a tricky situation. Nothing more.' She jumped up on the pretext of throwing a ball for Scarlet, her father's red setter, who had wandered on to the terrace in search of a game. 'But why are we wasting time talking about Piers?' she went on with her back to him.

'Because I have to be sure it *is* a waste of time. After you left Paris, I got to wondering why you'd changed your mind about me, after you'd turned me down flat at the château. And don't give me the old one about it being a woman's prerogative.'

Amanda swung round to him. 'Has all this erupted because I won't set a date for the wedding?'

'I'm not insisting you do. But I don't want to be kept dangling.'

Here was her chance to come clean, and conscience was impelling her to do so when Mrs Jones came out to say the taxi had arrived. Accepting the reprieve, Amanda determined to tell him when he came next weekend.

The matter was taken out of her hands by Lucien calling her from his office the following morning to say he was leaving for Australia the next day.

'Looks as if I'll be away six weeks at least. Our senior partner in Sydney has had a heart attack and I have to take over till we find a replacement. I suppose there's no chance of your coming with me?' he added wistfully.

'And have Liz cut my throat?'

'I feel like cutting hers!'

'Oh, Lucien.' Amanda writhed with guilt, yet could not bring herself to break their engagement so precipitately. She would have to work up to it.

'I'll miss you like hell,' he went on.

'Not once you get stuck into work.'

'I won't be so busy that I couldn't find time for you! What about joining me from South America?'

'You might have found a replacement for me by then,' she said, wishing with all her heart that he would. 'Australian girls are supposed to be stunning.'

'I know. Blonde, beautiful and bright. And you don't sound one bit jealous, whereas I'm working myself into a lather over those macho Brazilians and Argentinians you'll be meeting! I wish——' He broke off as someone spoke to him. 'Sorry, darling, but I must go. Stay well, sweetheart. I'll be in touch.'

'It's not a bad thing Lucien's going away,' her mother declared when she heard about his trip. 'It will give you both a chance to see each other in perspective.'

'You have doubts about him, then?'

'Only about his being the right man for you. I'm convinced you don't love him, my dear, so stop trying to fool me.'

In the face of such a command, Amanda had no choice but to come clean.

'You're right, Ma. I don't. And I'm going to tell him.'

'The sooner the better, I think. You can't get over one man by pretending you love another.'

'Get over?' Amanda quavered.

'Piers.' Lined grey eyes met unlined ones. 'He's marrying Hélène and you must accept it. Hiding behind Lucien wasn't sensible or necessary.'

'Was I that transparent?'

'Only to me.'

'Does Dad know?' Amanda asked after a pause.

'Don't be silly!' Mother and daughter exchanged wry glances, and the tension in the air evaporated.

Taking her mother's advice, Amanda sat down that night to write to Lucien. It was the most difficult letter she had ever penned, and after the fifth attempt she gave up and toyed with the notion of going to Paris to see him. Only the knowledge that he would be up to his ears preparing for his Australian trip decided her against it, and she was halfway through yet another letter when she knew that if she had any guts she would at least *talk* to him.

Although it was well past midnight, she dialled his number, her heart thumping so loudly that she could barely hear the ringing.

Then his voice came on the line, the alert tone telling her he was far from asleep. Not giving herself a chance to lose her courage, she rushed into speech.

'I'm sorry, Lucien, but I can't go through with it. I don't love you enough to marry you, and I was wrong to say I would. Please forgive me.'

'I'm the one who should be forgiven,' he said. 'You were on an emotional high when you came to see me in Paris, and I took advantage of it.'

'That isn't true.'

'Then let's say I swamped you with understanding—an emotion my friend Piers singularly lacked where you were concerned.'

'Piers and I never had that kind of relationship,' she said swiftly.

'Which is probably why you turned to me! But now you're back in your own skin and fitting it beautifully, you don't need me.'

'Lucien, I——'

'No, Amanda,' he interrupted. 'Don't make false promises. We're too adult for that.'

'You're r-right.' She couldn't keep the wobble from her voice. 'I'm truly sorry. I—I don't suppose we could stay friends, could we?'

'Of course we can. You'll always be special to me, my darling.'

'Oh, Lucien, I feel so badly.'

'Don't. I won't be entering a monastery because we're parting! Remember what you said about those stunning blondes in Sydney? Well, now I'll be free to put them on my hit list!'

She laughed, albeit shakily, and wondered what he would think if she asked him not to tell Piers they had broken their engagement. But she instantly dismissed the idea, knowing it would be a giveaway of her true feelings. Besides, what did it matter if Piers knew? These days relationships often ended as quickly as they had begun, with no hard feelings on either side, so the lighter she played the whole thing the better.

'I'll call you when I get back from Australia,' she heard Lucien say. 'I'm not scratching you from my little black book just yet!'

She laughed, and was deeply grateful he had made it so easy for her. Dear Lucien. She would never forget him.

Only as she replaced the receiver did she release her pent-up emotions and dissolve into a storm of weeping. Yet the tears were not so much for Lucien and herself as for Piers and the knowledge that, whoever she might share her future with, part of her heart would always belong to him.

Fortunately, the ensuing days were occupied finalising her plans for her South American trip. The long tour Liz had originally mooted had been whittled down to eighteen days of frenetic jet-hopping, and knowing she would be worn to a frazzle by the end of it, Amanda invited herself to stay with some cousins who lived on a ranch in Arizona.

It was the best thing she could have done, for, by the time she had flown between Rio, Buenos Aires, Lima and Cuzco, the quiet days spent basking out her fatigue in the hot dry sun of Arizona were more than welcome.

With the return of her energy came her restlessness, which she managed to stave off by pounding away at her articles on Cousin John's computer, which then, miracle of miracles, miraculously linked itself into the one in Liz's eighteenth-floor eyrie.

'Fantastic! Great!' came back the praise, followed by a personal call which left Amanda glowing. If nothing else, her career as a writer was secure. Trouble was, it was no compensation for losing Piers. Damn! She had promised herself not to think of him, yet the moment she let her mind float free, he came into it.

Sensing that she was less than happy, though they were too diplomatic to probe the reason, Cousin John and his wife, Annette, begged her to stay with them as long as she liked, and then proceeded to introduce her to every eligible bachelor within a hundred-mile radius—considered almost walking distance in the vastness of this state! And what eligible bachelors they were! Bronze-skinned and dynamic, they exuded a strength, energy and lust for life that left her breathless.

Yet not one of them left her more breathless than the rest, and though she had a marvellous time her inner self remained untouched.

'If I don't stop all this partying,' she told her cousins some three weeks later, 'I'll end up more exhausted than when I came!'

'You don't look in the least exhausted,' John drawled, his British accent still discernible even after years of living abroad.

'So much so,' Annette put in, 'that we want you to join us on a trip we've planned. In fact, we won't take "no" for an answer.'

Looking into Annette's cheerful face—eyes black as a raven's wing, hair white as a swan's—Amanda didn't have the heart to refuse. Extremely wealthy, though unfortunately childless, John and Annette happily 'adopted' all their friends' offspring, which made their home a fount of laughter and fun; a haven, too, as Amanda had gratefully found these past weeks.

'Where are we going?' she asked.

'Canada first. Then we'll just get in our jet and go where the mood takes us.'

Amanda capitulated. There was no urgency for her to return home, and the longer she stayed away the less she'd think of Piers.

Indeed, for the next month she barely thought of him, what with fishing off Victoria Island near Vancouver, riding alongside the wheat fields of Manitoba, climbing the lesser slopes of the Rockies, and then rounding it off with a paradisiacal boat trip through the Great Lakes.

'Count me out,' Amanda said when she heard John

order the jet to be prepared for take-off the following morning. 'It's time I went home.'

'You can't chicken out now,' he protested. 'The best part of the trip is yet to come.'

Wondering where the magic carpet was bound for, Amanda succumbed, a decision she bitterly regretted when, in the afternoon of the following day, their plane touched down at a private airfield in Northern California—in the Napa Valley of all places!

Mischievous fate, she thought as she stepped out and glimpsed the dark green vines in the far distance; all she needed was to bump into Piers. That would really put paid to her hope of forgetting him!

CHAPTER FIFTEEN

COINCIDENCE being what it is, Amanda was in no way surprised when, at the first party she went to with her cousins, the first man she saw as she walked ito the huge rectangular room overlooking the undulating Californian hills should be Piers, devastatingly handsome in dark slacks and white jacket that set off his bronze skin and silky black hair. Her throat went dry, her heart pounded and her legs faltered.

Luckily she was standing near a table, and she leaned against it for support, absorbing the look of his tall, supple body; dwelling a while longer on the finely chiselled mouth, and longer still on the strong-fingered hand that slowly moved up and down the length of his wine glass, the way—not so long ago—it had moved up and down her body, and she wondered whether her longing for him would ever abate.

True to form, he was the centre of a bevy of long-legged beauties with that special blonde Californian look, all glowing up at him with adoring eyes. Poor Hélène, having to marry a man like that! Amanda scowled, and in that instant Piers turned and saw her. That it was a shock to him she could tell by the sudden stillness which seemed to envelop him, almost as if he had been turned to stone. Or, better still, a pillar of salt! For he was his own Sodom and Gomorrah!

Tossing back her hair, she strolled across to him, glad she was looking her best in a shimmering silk organza Zandra Rhodes, the peacock colours giving added vibrancy to her lustrous auburn hair. She had grown it longer, and it was much curlier and reminiscent of Mandy's. But at least the colour was her own!

'Hello, Piers,' she said casually. 'Treading grapes in California?'

'With my bare feet,' he drawled, and, skilfully extricating himself from his admirers, steered her to a quieter corner of the room, leaving the hubbub of the crowd behind them, the Mancini music a gentle background to their conversation.

'I never expected to see *you* here,' he said.

'The party or California?'

'Both.'

'I had a pretty arduous assignment in South America, and decided to recuperate on my cousins' ranch in Arizona.'

One eyebrow rose. 'You're a long way from Arizona now.'

'Not when your run-about's a jet!'

'Those sort of cousins, eh?'

'The best kind to have,' she smiled. 'I take it you're staying at your vineyard?'

'Where else? Next to the château it's my favourite place. Hélène's too.'

Ostentatiously Amanda's eyes swept the room, and he gave a lazy grin. 'At the moment she's in Paris preparing for her wedding. At first it was going to be a small one, but like Topsy "it growed and growed".'

'Where's it being held? The Elysée Palace?'

His grin widened, but she noticed he did not answer. Perhaps he was afraid she was expecting an invitation? Come to think of it, it would be damned rude of him if he didn't invite her and her parents. Yet she had no intention of telling him, and searched wildly for something to say. But all she could think of was the man beside her and the fact that soon—she dared not ask how soon—he would be another woman's husband.

Surreptitiously she studied him from beneath her lashes. His face was thinner—gaunt, almost—and there were lines round his eyes she hadn't noticed before. Still, one couldn't burn the candle at both ends without its showing.

'I never did get to ask you,' she murmured, 'but was your mother very cross with me for deceiving her?'

'She was crosser with *me* for trying to pull the wool over her eyes. But she was highly amused when she heard how cleverly you'd pulled it over mine!' The corners of his mouth turned up. 'I deserved everything you did, Mandy—Amanda. If I remember rightly, I was pretty brutal when I first described you to Lucien. Am I forgiven?'

'Long ago,' she said lightly, and wondered what he would do if she flung herself into his arms and begged him not to marry Hélène.

'You must have had quite a laugh when I asked you to have an affair with me,' he went on.

'To be honest, I was disgusted.'

'Oh, by all means be honest,' he drawled. 'It makes a change between us, don't you think?'

She moved to the open window and breathed in the scented night air. 'I suppose I should have been flattered you fancied me, but all I felt was pity for Hélène.' Deliberately she faced him. 'You're a swine, Piers, and she's too good for you.'

'I agree.' A nerve twitched at his temple and he half-turned his head away. 'What would you say if I told you I intend being faithful to my wife?'

'I'd say you'd make a great comedy writer!'

'I mean it, though.'

'Then I'm glad for Hélène's sake.'

Amanda couldn't meet his eyes. It was an unbearable strain being so close to him, and she debated how soon she could decently move away. She breathed in deeply again to steady herself, but it had the opposite effect, for she could smell his after-shave and the special aroma of his skin.

'What's with you and Lucien?' he asked abruptly. 'Have you set a date yet?'

She was startled. 'Don't you know?'

'Obviously not. That's why I'm asking you.'

'No, no, I didn't mean that. What I meant is that we've called it off.'

He regarded her blankly, and it was several seconds before he spoke. 'I'm sorry. But no one told me. I came out here a week after you left Paris and I haven't heard from Lucien since. All I knew—and that came from a mutual friend—was that there were problems in his Australian office and he went there to settle them.'

'That's when we broke our engagement.'

'You mean *you* did,' Piers stated. 'I dined with him the night before I left France, and he didn't stop raving about you.'

'Don't make me feel guiltier than I already do,' she said with a deprecating laugh. 'I guess I'm fickle at heart. I couldn't bear the prospect of being tied down.'

'That's usually a man's line.'

She managed another smile. 'It was certainly yours long enough!'

'Not any more. I'm looking forward to settling down.'

'A good thing "Mandy" didn't take up your offer then,' she quipped, 'or she'd have been left high and dry!'

He shrugged. 'So what are your plans now?' he asked, clearly anxious to change the subject.

'To work and have fun.'

'You're a tease,' he said abruptly. 'And girls who play with fire are likely to get their fingers burned.'

'You think so?' She fluttered her lashes at him as

'Mandy' had done, and heard his sharp intake of breath.

'Stop that,' he said tersely. 'I'm no longer available.'

'My, my, a reformed rake!'

'Yes, as it so happens. Now may I get you a drink?'

'No, thanks. From the look on your face, you might poison it!'

Without answering, he turned on his heel and walked away.

Tears sprang to her eyes and she widened them in an effort to stop them spilling over, but several glittering drops trembled on her lower lashes, then rolled disconsolately down her cheek.

Piers ignored her for the rest of the evening, and, though she pretended to ignore him too, she couldn't help but be aware of the girls buzzing round him like bees round a honey jar, and was bitterly envious of the one he left with. Would he be taking her to bed? Bearing in mind his reputation, it seemed likely. He had said he intended being a faithful husband, but she'd take a bet he was a damned unfaithful fiancé!

The next few days Amanda did her best to forget Piers, but knowing he was close at hand made it impossible, and ruined what might otherwise have been an enjoyable stay in this most lovely part of California.

Driving along the broad, frequently empty roads, and seeing names like 'Domaine Chandon' and 'Krug', was like being in France, except that everything here was on a much larger scale.

What had initially been an experiment with a few vine cuttings from the 'Old Country' had become a major industry, and now many famous French *vignerons* were learning from the highly skilled techniques being used in this highly technical country. No hands were employed where a machine could do the job; wooden casks had given way to shiny steel vats—the temperatures controlled thermostatically—and the expert no longer relied solely on his 'nose' to blend a wine, for he could call on a welter of scientific expertise to back him up.

With her cousins she visited several wineries, and began to appreciate why the business held such a fascination for Piers. Producing good wine was like producing a healthy child, and required the same effort!

If she could have married him, how happily she would have shared this side of his life. It would have given them an extra bond, and one which he would not have with Hélène, who wished to follow her own career.

Stop thinking of Piers, she berated herself, and was overwhelmed by such desolation that she was hard put not to pack her bags and return to England there and then. But afraid that he might interpret her departure as a running away from him, she decided to stay another week and hope she would not bump into him.

Inevitably she did. In a restaurant—the Auberge du Soleil—where the food was as sensational as the view. Indeed, it seemed as if California was challenging France not only with wine, but with superb cuisine too.

Amanda and her cousins had dined leisurely at a table which gave them a panoramic view of the countryside dropping away below them. Replete and faintly woozy from too much excellent claret, Amanda felt more content than she had been in a long while, and was coming to the conclusion that she was getting over Piers, when he walked in with a woman and shattered her belief.

How puny he made every man seem! Pygmies all, compared with him. Yet what nonsense to think this when she was surrounded by scores of wide-shouldered, rangy Americans. But none of them had his sensual magnetism—a quality sensed by every female watching his progress through the room.

His table was in her direct line of vision, and she had far too good a view of him, and of his companion too, a strikingly attractive woman in her middle thirties, with whom he was deep in conversation. Though he gave the occasional smile, there was a serious air about him that told her their discussion was a business one.

The diners at the next table left, and in the intervening moments before it was occupied again Piers' attention wandered and he glanced around. He saw Amanda almost at once and, after a momentary hesitation, murmured something to his companion, then rose and came across to her.

Stiltedly she introduced him to John and Annette, and saw her cousin's look of dawning realisation.

'Dubray,' John murmured. 'Aren't you the third cousin who'll inherit from Henry?'

'Afraid so. A ridiculous situation, but there's nothing one can do about the law.'

'Will you live in the house when——?'

'John!' his wife protested, casting a glance at Amanda.

'Sorry, Amanda,' John apologised. 'It's hardly a topic you like hearing discussed!'

'Why don't you and your companion join us for coffee when you've finished dinner?' Annette put in diplomatically.

'It could be a while yet,' Piers replied, noting they were already at the coffee stage. 'I actually came over to ask if you were free to have lunch with me tomorrow at my winery.'

'We've seen so many,' Amanda began, 'that——'

'We'd love to,' Annette cut in enthusiastically.

'Good. I'll expect you about eleven. That will give

me time to show you round.' As he turned to go, he glanced at Amanda. 'I'll expect you, too.'

She smiled without replying, for she had no intention of going. She'd pretend a headache in the morning and cry off.

In the event there was no need for pretence, for a dream-filled night left her with a cracking head that set her reaching for the aspirin bottle.

'I'll call Piers and ask if he can make it another day,' Annette suggested.

'Please don't,' Amanda said hastily. 'You and John go and I'll sleep it off.'

'Piers will be awfully disappointed. I'm sure he only extended the invitation because he wanted to see *you*. I could tell from the way he looked at you.'

'Piers looks at all young women in that way,' Amanda muttered, lowering her lids and hoping Annette would take the hint and leave her.

Happily she did, and Amanda burrowed deeper into the pillows and prayed for oblivion. Eventually it came, and she was only wakened from it by the telephone several hours later. Lifting the receiver, she heard her mother's voice.

For an instant she was bemused. 'Where are you? What's wrong?'

'Nothing, dear, and I'm speaking from home. Where else would I be? I'm merely calling to see how you are and to find out when you'll be back. You seem to have been away ages.'

'I suppose so, with the time I spent in France as well.'

'Ah, France.' Her mother gave a little laugh. 'That reminds me. I spoke to Eliana last night.'

Amanda was fully awake now, instinct warning her this was why her mother had telephoned. 'Did Madame Dubray say anything about me? Piers told me she wasn't angry, but I didn't know whether to believe him.'

'You've seen him, then?'

'I bumped into him the first night I arrived here. In fact, John and Annette are lunching with him today, but I had a headache and couldn't go.'

'Really?'

'Yes, really!' There was silence at the other end. 'Mother, are you there?'

'Yes, dear.' There was a pause. 'It's merely that—well, I thought you'd like to know Hélène's getting married next month.'

The receiver slipped from Amanda's nerveless hand, and hurriedly she picked it up. 'So what?' she managed to say.

'So the man isn't Piers.'

'This is a very bad line,' Amanda mumbled.

'It's a very clear line, darling, and you haven't misheard me. Hélène is *not* marrying Piers, and was never going to!'

'Never going to?' Amanda croaked.

'According to Eliana, she's been engaged to a young doctor for the past year. But he was waiting to qualify before he married her.'

'Then why did Piers . . .? Oh, I don't believe it! It doesn't make sense!'

'It does, if you think about it.'

'What else did Madame Dubray tell you—and what did you say to *her*? Come on, Mother. Out with it.'

'I never said anything you wouldn't have wanted me to. I simply rang to see how she was, and naturally I asked about the wedding, which was when she said Piers wasn't even engaged! The rest you know.'

'You must have said *something* when she told you,' Amanda asserted.

'Only that I'd probably misunderstood you.'

'And?'

'Well—I—er—I did mention that you and Lucien had parted. But that wasn't a secret, was it?'

'No,' Amanda agreed. 'Piers knows anyway.' She frowned. 'I still can't fathom why he lied to me about Hélène.'

'Use your instincts, dear. Let your heart rule your head.'

'That isn't what mothers usually advise their daughters!'

With a laugh, her mother hung up, and Amanda lay back on the pillows, nowhere near as happy about the situation as her mother.

As far as she herself was concerned, there was only one reason why Piers had fabricated an engagement to Hélène: to keep Mandy at bay. Yet, if this were so, why had he then asked Mandy to have an affair with him?

Further cogitation gave Amanda the answer to this too. He had wanted to make 'Mandy' hate him. He had taken quite a gamble, she thought, for he would have been well and truly up the creek if 'Mandy' had agreed to become his girl friend! Amanda sighed. Knowing Piers' fertile imagination, she was sure he would have found a way out of that situation too.

So much for her mother's hopes that he had used Hélène for the self-same reason she herself had used Lucien.

Despondently she went to take a shower. The refreshing stream of water revived her spirits, and emerging from the glass cubicle she faced her reflection in the mirrored wall with a greater sense of well-being.

A slender, curvaceous redhead stared back at her, her tanned limbs glistening with dewy droplets of moisture, her nipples sharply pointed from the tingling spray. So had they firmed to Piers' touch, and with a moan of pain she flung the towel aside and buried her head in her hands.

She couldn't go on like this, her emotions fluctuating up and down like an elevator gone mad; somehow she had to come to grips with herself.

Dating other men hadn't helped, nor had arduous work. So what was her salvation? The sobering thought that time was the only healer decided her to return home.

Calmly she booked her flight, and discovering that the only one available left at eight the next morning, arranged to stay the night in San Francisco.

By the time her cousins returned to the hotel suite, Amanda had booked a room at the Mark Hopkins, and was packed and seated in the lounge, looking as cool and crisp as the Stag's Leap wine she was sipping.

'Such a shame you weren't able to come with us,' Annette commiserated. 'Piers gave us a wonderful day.'

'What did you do?' Amanda marvelled that she could appear so imperturbably interested.

'Well, after taking us round his home, which is absolutely sensational—a white hacienda with the most lovely Mexican furniture—we had a picnic lunch under the trees overlooking one of his vineyards.'

'It must have been quite a meal, considering it's already five o'clock!'

John laughed. 'We weren't eating all the time, old girl. Piers gave us so many wines to sample, we needed an hour with our feet up to recover!'

'I'm still quite tiddly,' Annette confided, lounging back in a chair. 'Would you mind awfully if we didn't go out to dinner tonight?'

'I won't be here to dinner,' Amanda admitted. 'I'm leaving for England in the morning and staying tonight in San Francisco.'

Neither John's nor Annette's protestations could make Amanda change her mind, and a couple of hours later, after affectionate goodbyes, she set off for the city in the car they had ordered for her.

This time tomorrow she would be thousands of miles from Piers, and, once she was, she would set about rebuilding her life.

CHAPTER SIXTEEN

It was barely nine o'clock when Amanda saw the lights of San Francisco twinkling ahead of her across an expanse of water, a sight that made her regret not giving herself a few days here to explore. She toyed with the notion of postponing her flight, then abandoned the idea. The haven of her home beckoned—almost as if she were returning to the comfort of the womb.

Once in her hotel room—with her nightdress and toiletries set out—she felt too restless to remain there and decided to go to Top of the Mark, the hotel's most famous bar, which afforded magnificent views of the city and bay.

Predictably, she had to queue for a table, and, though one soon became available in the centre of the room, she preferred to wait till another fell free beside a window.

She was on the verge of giving up when she finally got one, and with a half-bottle of champagne relaxed in her chair and allowed herself to be lulled by the rise and fall of the conversation around her. Several male eyes had watched her progress through the room, for even in the dim light her glistening auburn hair and full-breasted figure attracted attention. But her air of aloofness warded off any would-be companion, and in solitary isolation she sipped her champagne and watched the city lights twinkle and distort through misty eyes.

More and more people poured into the room: late-night diners to while away an hour before their meal, early diners to while away an hour after it. Air conditioning worked full blast to keep the atmosphere smoke-free and the skin goose-pimpled, and Amanda was glad of the soft mohair wrap she had thought to bring with her.

The laughter and buzz of talk grew louder as old habitués renewed acquaintance and new ones extolled the views. Ice clinked in glasses, waiters scurried to and fro, and the tinkle of piano keys rippled out a Golden Oldie whose sentimental lyrics, which would ordinarily have made Amanda laugh, now made her want to cry.

Finding her solitariness more than she could bear, she rose and left.

There was the inevitable crowd waiting at the elevators, and as one opened and disgorged a group of boisterous merrymakers she went to slip round them. A burly shoulder caught hers and sent her spinning back, and irritably she stepped forward again, only to find her way barred by a dark-clad figure. Blindly she sidestepped it, and not until she heard a sharp intake of breath did she look up and see it was Piers.

'You!' she exclaimed.

'You!' he echoed, and stepped back into the elevator with her. 'What are you doing here?'

'I'm staying the night on my way home. And you?'

'The same.' People were piling in, and Piers pulled her to the rear with him. 'Annette and John said you were ill.'

'It was only a headache,' she shrugged.

'You mean an excuse not to see me?'

'If you like.'

He moved to get out, then stopped. 'Have a drink with me?'

'I'm tired.'

'Rubbish!' He caught her arm and pulled her out of the elevator.

'What the hell do you think you're doing?' she hissed.

'Offering you a drink.'

'I don't want one. Anyway, I've already queued once, thank you very much, and——'

Whatever she had wanted to say was cut short by a smiling steward immediately leading them to a secluded table partially screened by plants.

'What it is to have influence,' she said sarcastically instead, as she sank into a chair.

'A tip ahead of time,' he explained drily, seating himself beside her. 'Now tell me, why the sudden departure for home?'

'It isn't sudden,' she lied. 'I booked days ago. Anyway, you're hardly the one to talk. You never said a word to Annette and John about *your* leaving!'

'Sharp, aren't you?'

'Part of my charm!'

'Actually, it is,' he said unexpectedly. 'You may be many things, Amanda, but you're not boring. In fact you're the most surprising girl I've met.'

'Then I'll surprise you some more by asking why you lied to me about Hélène.'

'Lied to you?'

'Come off it, Piers. My mother spoke to yours yesterday, and found out you were *never* engaged.'

'Aah. So that's why you're rushing back to London.'

She was confounded by the unexpectedness of his statement. 'What's my going to do with you and Hélène?'

'Perhaps knowing I'm free decided you to run.'

'From you?' she scoffed.

'Why not? After all, you're free too.' His eyes narrowed as if a thought had struck him, and he rose abruptly. 'Let's get out of here,' he ordered.

'What about my drink?'

'You didn't want one, remember?' Catching her arm, he propelled her smartly from the bar.

Elevator doors were about to close, and he wedged them inside even as they did.

'Where are we going?' she demanded.

He did not answer, though he leaned close to her whenever the elevator stopped at a floor, almost as if he knew she intended darting out when it reached hers. Indeed, as she made a move to do so at the fifteenth, he forcibly prevented her.

'Oh no, you don't,' he breathed in her ear. 'We've a few things to discuss first.'

The next floor was his, and he marched her along the corridor to his room, retaining his hold on her with one hand while unlocking the door with the other.

'You don't have to clutch at me,' she grumbled, playing it cool. 'I won't run off. If you want to talk, we'll talk.'

He swung open the door and she nonchalantly followed him into his bedroom—a replica of her own, even to the toiletries on the dressing table and night things laid out on the bed.

'Why the smile?' he asked, seeing her eyes take them in.

'I'm amused at how similar people can be when they travel.'

'Perhaps we don't take enough account of our similarities,' he said jerkily. 'A nightgown instead of pyjamas, Givenchy instead of 'Joy', and Lucien in place of Hélène.' His lids lifted, impaling her with a piercing blue gaze. 'You get my meaning, Amanda?'

All too clearly she did, and silently cursed him for his astuteness. The last thing she wanted was his sympathy, and if he went on exploring this particular avenue, that's what she'd get. Her hands grew damp, as did the shadowy cleft between her breasts, and she drew a jerky breath, straining the jade silk blouse across them.

His eyes instantly lowered to their fullness. 'Your breasts always give you away, Amanda. Small and pointed when you're angry, full and rounded when you're happy.'

'Be careful I don't start analysing *you*,' she said furiously, 'or you might be embarrassed!'

'Never with you, Amanda. Those days are gone.'

'Gone?' She inched towards the door, and though he saw it he made no move to stop her.

'Gone,' he reiterated. 'Because the moment you told me you were going back to England, and then said you knew my engagement was phoney, a great cloud lifted from my life, or maybe I should say the wool lifted from my eyes.'

'I don't know what you're talking about.'

'Liar!'

He slipped off his jacket and went to hang it in the hall cupboard, remaining there effectively to block her exit. The fine cambric of his white shirt revealed the curly black hairs on his chest, and she hastily looked away.

'Know something?' he went on softly. 'I believe your engagement to Lucien was as phoney as mine to Hélène, and made for similar reasons.'

'Really?' she said with heavy sarcasm.

'Yes, really. In the beginning I used Hélène as a shield because I knew 'Mandy' was attracted to me, and I wanted to warn her off.'

'How thoughtful of you!'

'I happen to think it was,' he said. 'But then afterwards I needed a shield for a different reason. You see, Hélène helped me to hide my real feelings for "Mandy".'

'Oh?' Amanda said in a thin voice.

'Don't tell me "Mandy" didn't know I was sexually attracted to her?'

'That was clear as a lighthouse beam!'

'But it soon became more than a sexual need,' he went on as if he hadn't heard her. 'I started wondering what future we could have together, how happy she'd be living my sort of life, and whether I had the temperament to cope with her. Dammit, Amanda!

You've no idea how that dreadful accent and grammar of yours tried my temper. To say nothing of that raucous laugh!'

It was impossible for her not to laugh now, her own natural, honeyed sound, and he gave a rueful smile.

'You may well be amused, you witch. But if you knew the hell you put me through . . .'

'You deserved it all.'

'Not quite all. That night when I came to your room and we made love, I——'

'We didn't!'

'Not quite,' he said huskily, 'but as near as made no difference. Certainly near enough for me to realise I couldn't give "Mandy" up no matter what.'

'Despite the rotten grammar and raucous laugh?'

'Despite everything,' he said soberly. 'I was on the verge of asking her to marry me, but was scared she was more bowled over by what I had to offer than by me.'

'How did you intend finding out how "Mandy" really felt?' Amanda asked.

'I intended taking her to California with me. I figured if we could be happy together in a quiet, countrified life—for that's the way I live here—then we'd have a chance of making a go of marriage. I also wanted to show "Mandy" I wasn't the playboy she assumed me to be—well, not for the past five years, anyway.'

Though Amanda could appreciate his reasoning, she still didn't understand why he had persisted with the Hélène charade once he'd realised his true feelings. But even as she went to ask him, he pre-empted the question.

'When my mother informed me Hélène was coming to the château, I already knew your true identity.'

'*What?*' Amanda gaped at him. This was totally unexpected, and changed so many things that she could not begin to take them in.

'When I left your bedroom that night,' he went on, 'my mother came to tell me she'd had a call from Margaret Herbert. Seems your mother was worried because you were away so long, and called mine for a diplomatic chat.'

'You mean she let the cat out of the bag?'

'Not at first. But I gather mine had a quiet moan about the "sweet but totally unsuitable girl I'd fallen for", and your parent took pity on her and told her the truth!' Piers left the hallway for his room, as if no longer worried that Amanda would make a dash for freedom. 'You should have anticipated it, you know. You couldn't expect your mother to let you go on making a fool of mine indefinitely.'

'I'd no intention of doing it indefinitely. As soon as I'd got you to propose to "Mandy", I intended coming clean.'

'You mean you planned to laugh in my face and walk out?'

'Something like that,' she said, hoping he wouldn't guess how quickly that intention had changed. 'Of course, now I see why you went into that fantastic act with Hélène,' she continued, 'though I'm dying to know how you got the chance to put her in the picture? From the minute your mother told you she was coming to the château, I stuck to you like a leech.'

'I signalled my mother to speak to her!' Piers couldn't restrain a grin as Amanda, who hadn't even considered that aspect, collapsed on to the nearest chair.

'How cunning of you! Well, you certainly won *that* round!'

'Not before time, either! You see, I wanted to teach you a lesson. Don't forget I'd already planned to take "Mandy" to California with me, and discovering she was Amanda Herbert gave me the biggest shock of my life.' His eyes deepened with the memory. 'I could

have shaken that lovely head of yours till your teeth
fell out!'

'Poor Piers.' Amanda's voice was soft with sympathy, but her lips were curling with mirth.

'Not poor for long, though. I soon saw the funny
side of it and had a good laugh. And that's when I
decided to play you at your own game for a while.
Hélène's arrival next day—which I hadn't expected—
played straight into my hands. In fact, it was her idea
that I asked you to have an affair with me after I'd
supposedly married her. You should have seen your
face when I did!'

'You should have seen *yours* when I turned you
down!' Amanda whipped back.

'It wasn't the turning down that knocked me for
six,' Piers stated. 'It was learning you were going to
marry Lucien . . .'

His voice trailed away, but Amanda said nothing.
Happiness was seeping into her every pore, yet she
was scared to trust it, scared she wanted Piers so
desperately that she was reading more into his words
than was there.

He walked away from her and looked out at the
skyline, and she gazed at his erect head, the crisp black
hair, the proud stance of his lithe body. In tapering
trousers and tight-fitting shirt that showed the ripple
of every muscle, he could have made the centrefold of
Cosmopolitan, and would, without question, be the
centre of her life for a long time to come, even if she
never saw him again.

Never see him again? She was crazy to think that!
Hadn't he just said he loved her? That he had loved
her as 'Mandy' and would have married her the
instant he was sure 'Mandy' loved him!

Jumping up, she went to stand beside him, her step
so light that he was unaware of her proximity until he
saw the reflection of her hands in the window as they
came to clasp him and draw him back against her.

'I used Lucien as a buffer,' she whispered, 'and I only hope he'll forgive me. But it has always and only been you. Never anyone else.'

He turned within the circle of her arms and placed his around her, drawing her close so that she could feel the tension of his body. As her hands moved up his back and across his shoulders, she felt him relax, but only a little, almost as if he were afraid to believe she was in his arms, loving at last.

'I was so jealous of Lucien,' he groaned, his mouth pressed to her temple. 'You don't know the sleepless nights I suffered picturing you in his arms, held close to you like this!'

He pressed her tighter to him, his throbbing body making further explanations unnecessary. And indeed there was no chance for words, for his mouth found hers with urgency and drained the sweetness within, as though parched for it. And all the while his hands roamed over her, those long supple hands that she loved: feathering her body, hovering over the secret recesses to skim them lightly.

'So many clothes,' he breathed, and answering his unspoken plea she withdrew her mouth and, inches apart from him, unbuttoned her blouse and slipped it off, then stepped out of her skirt. Her passion-filled breasts overflowed the wisp of lace attempting to confine them, and with a careless shrug she unhooked it and let it fall, leaving only a triangle of silk to cover the burning triangle of her desire.

Even as her hands went to the silk, Piers stopped her, running a trembling finger along the inside of the ruching. A curl of fire spiralled in the pit of her stomach, and, feeling its quiver, he sought its site, his palm rough against the satiny smoothness of her skin.

Like a snake sloughing its skin, her panties slithered to the floor, and she stood before him in all the glory of her ripe womanhood, unashamedly ready for him. Their eyes locked, and she saw the flame of passion burning bright in the blue. There was the sound of buttons tearing, the swift burr of a zip, then Piers, a black-haired Adonis, picked her up effortlessly and carried her to the bed.

Arms entwined about his neck, she clung to him as he flung aside the covers and came down with her upon the sheet.

It felt cool against her back, though a fire raged on top of her as Piers pressed his body the length of hers, his weight supported by his arms, yet so close that nipple brushed against nipple, stomach curved into stomach, hair curled into hair.

'Lie still, Amanda,' he pleaded. 'I've wanted this so long, I want it to go on for ever.'

But how could she listen to him when every limb, every nerve, ached and throbbed for him? She was already his in mind, and longed to be his in body; would never know peace until she was.

Her thighs parted and he slipped between them, his own thighs taking his weight and leaving his hands free to roam. Unerringly they found her breasts, cupping them and lifting their fullness, the better to suck the nipples. Desire rose in her like a flame, and she gasped and cried his name, pulling his head down closer.

'I love you,' she murmured into the silken dark hair. 'Oh, Piers, how I love you!'

She wrapped her legs around him, the movement inviting him into her, and instantly the shaft of his manhood thrust forward in an uncontrollable burst of passion, piercing through the protective folds to the deep, inner core of her being, thrust after thrust sending him higher and higher inside her. With cries of her own need, she responded, her muscles relaxing to accept him, then tightening to hold him secure, drawing from him his every drop of life-giving moisture.

'I love you, I love you,' he gasped, and together

they reached a shuddering climax that held them suspended from time and thought, floating on a sea of satiation that rocked them finally into peace.

Limb entwined with limb, they lay quiet till strength returned, and Piers, exultant now, yet strangely humble, cradled Amanda close and pledged his life to hers.

'Don't play games with me any more,' he murmured. 'Our marriage must be a partnership, not a contest.'

'It will,' she assured him, and, remembering how nearly she could have missed seeing him tonight, gave a little cry of panic. 'If we hadn't been staying in the same hotel, I'd never have seen you again.'

'Don't you believe it. Once I'd got over my hurt pride, I'd have come to you on bended knees.'

'But you were leaving for France without even saying goodbye!'

'When you didn't come to lunch today, I was sure you despised me so much you couldn't bear to see me. And that made me so angry with myself, I decided to fly home to think things out.'

'I thought only women ran back to Mummy!'

He laughed. 'Weren't you doing the same?'

'Yes!' A pink-tipped finger delicately caressed his stomach. The muscles contracted and she moved her hand lower, to have it caught and held by his. 'No?' she whispered.

'Not till you've answered my question.'

'What question?'

'Will you marry me, Mandy Amanda, and be the bane of my life, the light of my soul?'

'Yes, yes, yes!' she cried.

Joyously he laughed, a deep rumbling sound that echoed in her ears as she lay upon his chest.

'We're about to make three people very happy,' he murmured.

'And two more ecstatic,' she added.

'Two more?'

'You and me!'

He chuckled. 'How long will it take you to buy a trousseau?'

'As long as it will take you to get a licence!'

'You mean you don't want a big white wedding with a thousand guests?'

'I want only *you*,' she said softly, 'and the quickest, quietest wedding possible.'

'With the longest, slowest honeymoon,' he answered, lifting her bodily on top of him. 'Just like this,' he explained, moving his hands slowly up and down her. 'Just like this.'

Harlequin Presents

Coming Next Month

959 THE CALL OF HOME Melinda Cross
After her father's death and her mother's recovery from her breakdown, an American painter returns to her childhood haunt to heal her own wounds—and comes up against a man who's as much in need of love as she is.

960 WOMAN OF HONOUR Emma Darcy
Labeled a home-wrecker when a certain lawyer's brother-in-law neglected to mention his marriage, an Australian chef turns workaholic. But guess who her next Dial-A-Dinner Party client is?

961 TRY TO REMEMBER Vanessa James
A distraught amnesiac and a forceful merchant banker search from Devon to Morroco for something to jolt her memory. But what really knocks her for a loop is her feelings for him.

962 A MAN POSSESSED Penny Jordan
Fate brings an old friend of a widow's late husband back into her life, the man who'd rejected her in the midst of her bleak marriage. But it seems he'd desired her, after all.

963 PASSIONATE VENGEANCE Margaret Mayo
A London designer finds herself fired on trumped-up charges. Her reputation's smeared. So the job at Warrender's Shoes seems like a lifeline—until she discovers her boss's motives in hiring her.

964 BACHELOR IN PARADISE Elizabeth Oldfield
The soap opera star a British author interviews in Florida isn't the vain celebrity she'd expected. He lives frugally, disappears every Wednesday, declares parts of his life "off-limits"—and fascinates her to no end!

965 THE ARRANGEMENT Betsy Page
Marry the woman from Maine or forfeit control of the family business, an uppercrust Bostonian warns his son. But the prospective bride is as appalled by the arrangement as the groom—so they have one thing in common, at least.

966 LOVE IN THE MOONLIGHT Lilian Peake
A young journalist wants to warn her sister in Cornwall that the man she's dallying with is a heartbreaker. But how can she—when she's still in love with the man herself?

Available in March wherever paperback books are sold, or through Harlequin Reader Service:

In the U.S.
P.O. Box 1397
Buffalo, N.Y.
14240-1397

In Canada
P.O. Box 603
Fort Erie, Ontario
L2A 5X3

Take 4 best-selling love stories FREE
Plus get a FREE surprise gift!

Six exciting series for you every month... from Harlequin

Harlequin Romance·
The series that started it all

Tender, captivating and heartwarming...
love stories that sweep you off to faraway places
and delight you with the magic of love.

◆

Harlequin Presents·
Powerful contemporary love stories...as individual as the women who read them

The No. 1 romance series...
exciting love stories for you, the woman of today...
a rare blend of passion and dramatic realism.

◆

Harlequin Superromance®
It's more than romance...
it's Harlequin Superromance

A sophisticated, contemporary romance-fiction
series, providing you with a longer,
more involving read...a richer mix of complex plots,
realism and adventure.

Harlequin
American Romance™
Harlequin celebrates the
American woman...

...by offering you romance stories written
about American women, by American women
for American women. This series offers you
contemporary romances uniquely North American
in flavor and appeal.

◆

Harlequin Temptation
Passionate stories for
today's woman

An exciting series of sensual, mature stories of
love...dilemmas, choices, resolutions...
all contemporary issues dealt with in a true-to-life
fashion by some of your favorite authors.

◆

Harlequin Intrigue
Because romance can be quite
an adventure

Harlequin Intrigue, an innovative series that
blends the romance you expect...
with the unexpected. Each story has an added
element of intrigue that provides a new twist to
the Harlequin tradition of romance excellence.

Harlequin Books·

PROD-A-2

HARLEQUIN HISTORICAL

Explore love with Harlequin in the Middle
Ages, the Renaissance, in the Regency, the
Victorian and other eras.

Relive within these books the endless ages of
romance, set against authentic historical
backgrounds. Two new historical love stories
published each month.

HIST-B-1